"Who

"Maybe you shouldn't want to know."

Gabe was sure that was true. He shouldn't try to open Pandora's box. He might never get Sabrina put back inside, where she couldn't wreak havoc with his senses, stir his hormones—make him want what he shouldn't have.

When her voice came, it was low. And soft. And very, very sexy.

"I'm not really a puzzle, you know. What you see is what I am."

"And what is that?"

"I'm a student of research. I like things clear and concise."

He leaned forward, searching her eyes. "What about Sabrina, the woman? What does she like?"

Dear Reader,

Love is always in the air at Silhouette Romance. But this month, it might take a while for the characters of May's stunning lineup to figure that out! Here's what some of them have to say:

"I've just found out the birth mother of my son is back in town. What's a protective single dad to do?"—FABULOUS FATHER Jared O'Neal in Anne Peters's *My Baby, Your Son*

"What was I thinking, inviting a perfect—albeit beautiful—stranger to stay at my house?"—member of THE SINGLE DADDY CLUB, Reece Newton, from *Beauty and the Bachelor Dad* by Donna Clayton

"I've got one last chance to keep my ranch but it means agreeing to marry a man I hardly know!"—Rose Murdock from *The Rancher's Bride* by Stella Bagwell, part of her TWINS ON THE DOORSTEP miniseries

"Would you believe my little white lie of a fiancé just showed up—and he's better than I ever imagined!" —Ellen Rhoades, one of our SURPRISE BRIDES in Myrna Mackenzie's *The Secret Groom*

"I will not allow my search for a bride to be waylaid by that attractive, but totally unsuitable, redhead again!"—sexy rancher Rafe McMasters in *Cowboy Seeks Perfect Wife* by Linda Lewis

"We know Sabrina would be the perfect mom for us—we just have to convince Dad to marry her!"—the precocious twins from Gayle Kaye's *Daddyhood*

Happy Reading!

Melissa Senate
Senior Editor

Please address questions and book requests to:
Silhouette Reader Service
U.S.: 3010 Walden Ave., P.O. Box 1325, Buffalo, NY 14269
Canadian: P.O. Box 609, Fort Erie, Ont. L2A 5X3

DADDYHOOD

Gayle Kaye

Silhouette
ROMANCE™
Published by Silhouette Books
America's Publisher of Contemporary Romance

To my brother, my friend, Gary Sondergard—
thanks for sharing my childhood.
And to my own little charmers,
Diane and Cathy, who inspired this book.
Love and hugs.

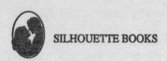 SILHOUETTE BOOKS

ISBN 0-373-19227-4

DADDYHOOD

Copyright © 1997 by Gayle Kasper

Printed in U.S.A.

Books by Gayle Kaye

Silhouette Romance

Hard Hat and Lace #925
His Delicate Condition #961
Daddy Trouble #1014
Bachelor Cop #1177
Daddyhood #1227

GAYLE KAYE

had a varied and interesting career as an R.N. before finally hanging up her stethoscope to write romances. She indulges this passion in Kansas City, Missouri, where she lives with her husband and one very spoiled poodle. Her first romance in 1987 reached the finals of the Romance Writers of America Golden Heart contest.

When she's not writing, she loves to travel or just curl up with a good book.

SABRINA'S "BY-THE-BOOK RULES"
(GABE'S "ON-THE-JOB" DADDY DO'S AND DON'TS)
FOR RAISING TWINS

1) Twins should never be dressed alike, so as to encourage their individuality.
   But they'll probably choose to dress the same "individual way" on the same day!

2) It is best to avoid cutesy or rhyming names when naming twins.
   But with the cost of "doubling" everything, it helps to have the same monogram!

3) For birthdays and other gift-giving occasions, give each twin her own unique and individual gift!
   But you'd better pick up a spare of everything!

4) Encourage a natural rivalry between twins and choose activities that channel their competitiveness.
   Huh? But who gets to clean up after such "competitiveness"?

5) Take time separately with each twin so that she knows she is loved for herself.
   Agreed! Each twin needs lots of individual love. But—hint to Sabrina—so does their daddy!

Prologue

"Is not."

"Is too."

"Is not."

"*Dad...!*"

The twins were fighting again. Gabe Lawrence took the cake he was baking for their sixth birthday out of the oven. It was to be a three-tiered job, with lots of fluffy icing between the layers.

But as he flopped the round layer pans onto the kitchen countertop, he sighed at the sinkholes in the center of each. He probably should have bought a cake. But he was determined to be a hands-on dad.

Was this penance for the years he hadn't been?

He took off the oven mitts, tossing them beside the sorry cake layers, and went to settle his daughters' dispute.

"Dad, she's got my Barbie and won't give it

back,'' Hannah said the moment he stepped into the playroom, the one that used to be his home office.

"It's *my* Barbie. Nana gave it to me—just me!" Heather retaliated, at which time each girl grabbed a leg and pulled, snapping the poor doll's legs like a wishbone.

That really set up a howl.

"Okay, princesses, stop your crying and I'll see if I can...perform doll surgery. Okay?"

That brought a snuffle and a sob and wide-eyed hopefulness from each girl.

"Then she can't play with it anymore. Isn't that right, Dad?" Hannah said.

"No one will be playing with Barbie," he informed them. "She'll need about six weeks to convalesce."

Maybe in that time he would have decided which twin had ownership.

"What's con...con...v'lesce?" Heather asked.

"It's— Never mind, sweethearts. Just try to play. *Without fighting*—okay?"

Two sets of bright blue eyes peered up at him through long, fringed lashes. Small rosebud-pink mouths pursed into appealing pouts. Gabe considered his look-alikes' small cherubic faces, full of sweet innocence, but he suspected it was only a matter of time before there'd be a new squabble between them.

He confiscated the Barbie parts and frowned, wondering if he'd made a mistake turning down his sister's offer to come and help with the twins. But he knew he hadn't. The girls were his—and he loved them. He'd get the hang of this fathering thing.

Somehow.

He ruffled their blond curls and tweaked their pert upturned noses, which made them both giggle. In minutes they were playing again—quietly, this time. Gabe made his way out of the room and into the den, sinking into his favorite overstuffed chair.

The twins were still adjusting to life here with him. It had been six months since the accident that had killed their mother, Gabe's ex-wife. Meg had been a terrific mom, but *he* hadn't always been the best dad in the world…and he was sorry about that. He wasn't sure one inexperienced father could make things right again for two little girls, but if love counted for anything, they would all weather this.

He might not be experienced at child rearing but he was getting plenty of advice—from every female in the family and from the women in the neighborhood. One had even sent him a book on the subject of raising twins, a wordy tome by the renowned child psychologist, Dr. Sabrina Moore.

He unearthed the dog-eared copy from beneath a stack of kiddie books on the end table beside him. Gabe had read the book—or rather, *tried* to read it. It was a real snoozer, full of facts and figures and theories that he wondered if the lofty Dr. Moore had ever put to the test.

Somewhere besides a clinical lab, that is.

He scanned the glossy photo of her on the back cover. She was pretty, in a soft, don't-touch sort of way. A brunette. With long, silky hair that barely brushed her shoulders squared for the picture. Her smile looked posed—and he wondered what it would take to make the lady smile like she meant it. Her silk blouse with its high neck didn't do much for a man's libido, but still he had the feeling there was a lot of sensual woman beneath that prim facade.

Not that Gabe had any business being curious.

The only women he had time for in his life right now were two soon-to-be six-year-olds who needed him. Which brought him back to the problem of the twins' sibling rivalry.

He flipped the book over and thumbed through the pages, wondering just what intellectual *theories* the intriguing Dr. Moore had to offer on the subject....

Chapter One

Dr. Sabrina Moore glanced out over her audience in the small community-college auditorium, smiling at the group of young moms, and one dad, who sat listening to her. The *dad* had come in late, looking harried and restless as he sat in the back row, somewhat apart from the others.

In seven cities around the country in as many days, she'd given this discussion on the joys and problems of raising twins, promoting her new book, *Multiples*. The text was a compilation of her years researching twins, triplets, even quadruplets and one rare set of quints.

She'd saved her final round of talks on her busy tour for Denver—her home—and she was glad to be back. The tour had proved tiring and stressful and she wanted nothing more than to unwind.

Her gaze went to the man in the back row again.

In his right hand he clutched a copy of her book, and a little thrill of excitement rippled through her. She shifted in her chair, fully expecting him to come up afterward and ask her to autograph it for him, or maybe for his wife.

She was still having a little trouble getting used to all this fame and attention. She'd devoted so much of her life to research, had hidden herself away in quiet, *safe,* academia for so long, she'd forgotten there was a real world out there.

Shuffling her notes, she went on with her talk, trying to keep her attention off the man in the last row and on the subject at hand. Maybe it was because she had so few men sit in on her sessions that he garnered her attention.

Or maybe it was that he was such a handsome specimen of fatherhood, with a strong square jaw and hair the nut-brown color of an acorn. He wore it slightly long, just brushing the collar of his light blue shirt that stretched across impossibly broad shoulders.

It wasn't like Sabrina to scrutinize her audience—she'd never done it before now—and she tore her gaze away, concentrating on the group closer to the front.

Questions and answers followed the discussion, along with a brisk sale of copies of her book—which was the reason she was there, after all. That and to share the knowledge of her extensive research.

Her work at the Sherwood Institute was important to her. In fact, since her marriage fell apart a year ago, it had been everything to her. The one bright spot in her life, the one constant, and she poured her heart and soul into it. All her energies.

Sabrina spoke a friendly word to the last mother who'd come forward to purchase her book, remembering the woman had told her at the beginning of the session that she and her husband were the proud parents of triplets, a result of fertility drugs.

With the advent of fertility medications, more and more multiple births were occurring than normally did in nature—which made Sabrina's research on the subject that much more vital.

As the woman trailed out, Sabrina moved to gather together her discussion materials and deposit them in her briefcase.

"Interesting theories, Dr. Moore."

Sabrina nearly dropped her charts and graphs at the low male voice that rumbled so close beside her. She knew without glancing up to whom it belonged. She'd been so busy talking with the last few mothers that she'd forgotten all about the solitary dad occupying a seat in the back row. His deep resonant greeting, however, brought her sense of recall to vivid life.

When she looked up, blue eyes met her gaze. Not just any ordinary shade of blue, but a cool, glittering sapphire. Up close he was even more intriguing, not to mention daunting. For a moment she felt unnerved, but only for a moment.

She lifted her chin. "Thank you. I'm glad you liked them."

His gaze took her in—a slow, thorough assessment that unnerved her all over again. "Oh, I didn't say I liked them, I said I found your theories *interesting*. There's a world of difference."

Was there something the man didn't understand about her discussion? It was all there in her book, which he'd obviously read, given the dog-eared condition of it.

She finished stuffing her charts and graphs inside her briefcase, and gave him a smile. "Did you have a question about some point I made, Mr....?"

He gave her a smile, too. Albeit a small one, it did wonderful things to those blue eyes. She read a wisdom in them, one that comes from living life and not having it turn out exactly to your liking. Sabrina knew all about that—and she didn't ever want to run the gauntlet again.

"Gabe Lawrence," he supplied. "And I don't have a question. I have a comment."

"And that is...?"

Gabe had found the woman far prettier than her picture. A beauty, in fact, with green almond-shaped eyes that were far too sultry—and a definite counterpoint to that starched, bookish look she seemed to hide behind. He could go easy on her, but that had never been his style.

He dropped the book on the speaker's table in front of her. "Your theories, Dr. Moore, are a lot of hooey."

"Hooey?"

She spoke the word like it were not in her vocabulary, her lips cupping it and forming something akin to a pucker as she did so, lips he'd consider kissing if it were the right time or place. Her green eyes sparked with silent fury, a warning he should back off. "Psychobabble, Dr. Moore."

"I know the meaning of the word, Mr. Lawrence. But perhaps you could be a bit more specific than psychobabble or...*hooey*."

There went that pucker again. It heated his insides in a way he wished it didn't.

"Happily," he replied. He'd go with a small point first. "You stated that twins should never be dressed alike. 'It thwarts their individuality,' I believe were your exact words."

"I know what I said—and I stick by my theory," she added emphatically.

Gabe wondered if she knew that twins were sometimes frightened, that sometimes there was comfort in pairs. Hannah and Heather had lost their mother recently—dressing alike gave them a sense of belonging, at least to each other. He wished they felt they belonged to him, as well—but that would come in time.

He hoped.

"It so happens, Doctor, that my twins *like* to dress alike. If one has a big pink bow in her hair, the other wants one, too. Same holds true for lacy socks or pink sundresses," he added.

"Just a regular pair of little bookends, aren't they?"

Gabe hadn't missed the hint of sarcasm in her low, soft voice or the way her chin had raised when she'd delivered her comeback. She obviously wasn't a woman who could be backed into a corner easily. "No need to get all prickly, Doctor. It's just a practical fact—*practical* being the key word here. Something that was noticeably absent in those theories of yours."

She gazed up at him, her green eyes soft and silvery in the overhead light. "Do you do this often, Mr. Lawrence?"

"What—point out the error of someone's ways?"

That, too, Sabrina thought. "No—sound so opinionated."

He struck Sabrina as the kind of man who'd leave the parenting to his wife. In fact, she'd be willing to bet six months of her royalties on it. Still, she had to admit, he *had* come here to her talk—though he seemed to have missed the whole point of it.

He smiled. "Only when I believe strongly in something."

"Well, I'd really love to stay and debate the practicality of my theories with you further, but I can't right now." She paused. "I'm giving a second talk here next week. Perhaps you and your wife would care to attend. You might even *learn* something."

"I don't have a wife."

She'd picked up her briefcase and taken a step toward the door. Now she stopped and turned back to him. A single father struggling with twins. That could make an interesting sidebar to her research, but she quickly checked that thought. Not with this man, who made her all too aware of her femininity. And found fault with her carefully researched theories.

"I'm sorry. I didn't know."

"Because I hadn't told you," he offered.

"Well, then...perhaps you'd like to attend the session," she added. "It'll be a more in-depth—"

"I doubt that."

"Doubt that you'll attend?"

"Doubt that it'll be more *in-depth*. I read your book, Dr. Moore. Cover to cover. You don't go in depth on any point."

Sabrina's spine grew ruler straight. What did this man know about her work, her theories? "For your information, Mr. Lawrence," she said emphatically, "that book was the culmination of five years of painstaking research, five years of dedicated study of child development. I have not one, but two—count 'em—*two* doctorates. I've taught countless seminars on the subject and have just finished a speaking tour around the country."

He gave her a slow, thorough smile. "Yeah, well, that may be, Doctor. But have you ever seen a pair of twins *up close and personal?*"

"What?"

"You heard me. How many twins have you spent time with? Not studying them like a scientist would an interesting bug, but putting a ribbon in their hair, listening to their squabbles, drying their tears when they cry?"

Gabe watched her pretty mouth open, then close around whatever angry rebuttal she'd been about to toss his way. "That's what I figured," he answered smugly at her nonanswer.

She ducked her head and, clutching her briefcase, stormed through the doorway and down the hall, the firm click of her sexy high heels tapping a staccato beat against the tile floor.

Maybe he'd come on a little too strong—one of his less flattering habits, Gabe knew. "Hey, wait up," he said and tailed after her.

"Look, I'm sorry," he allowed when he'd caught up with her. "I didn't mean my comment as a *total* criticism of your book."

"Of course not." She kept on walking. Down the hall and out the door into the bright early-afternoon sun. She didn't even slow, just made for the parking lot and her small, sensible blue-gray car parked there.

Gabe kept pace beside her. "Look, maybe we can discuss this."

She kept walking. "I'm a busy woman, Mr. Lawrence. Now, if you'll excuse me." She reached for the door handle of her car.

"Then meet the twins. I promise you, you'll learn a thing or two." She'd learn just how silly a few of her well-thought-out theories really were. She'd learn how Gabe dealt with the realities of twins on a daily basis. She'd learn she didn't have *all* the answers.

But the woman didn't jump at his invitation. She only handed him a glower that could have buried a lesser man beneath the parking lot.

Gabe was *not* a lesser man.

"You surprise me, Dr. Moore. I thought you were woman enough to accept a challenge."

She paused, tapping her fingers on the door handle of her car. "And just what challenge might that be?"

"Meet one cute little set of twins, head-on. Hannah and Heather," he said. "I might be partial about the cute part, but then I'm their father."

Hannah and Heather—at least it wasn't rhyming names, Sabrina thought. She'd devoted a whole chapter of her book to what *that* did to siblings. She'd have to give him credit though for his fatherly pride.

"Look, I'm taking them for pizza tonight. Join us. Antonio's—it's their favorite place."

"I—I have plans this evening," she told him and opened her car door.

"Then how about tomorrow night? It's the twins' sixth birthday and I'm throwing a party for them. Cake, birthday punch, dinner."

"A birthday party...?"

"Yes."

Why was she hesitating? Why hadn't she hopped in her car and roared off, leaving Gabe Lawrence standing in the dust, with nothing to do but stare at her retreating back bumper?

Because he'd appealed to her on some level beside just the feminine? Called out to her scholarly side— the side that was curious about two sweet little girls who had a bonehead for a father?

She knew that it was.

And perhaps, just perhaps, she wanted to recover the reputation the man had so effectively taken aim at.

His planned birthday party sounded safe—well, safe enough. And she did want to meet the twins.

"I just may take you up on it, Mr. Lawrence. But—it's certainly not because of your charm."

The smile her double-edged acceptance put on his lips had a part of her doubting the wisdom of what she'd just done.

The part that could get hurt....

Sabrina glanced again at the suburban address on the tan-colored business card with crisp black lettering that Gabe Lawrence had given her. According to the card, he ran Lawrence Advertising, and his office address was the same as his home. An arrangement that enabled him to stay close to his twin daughters? she wondered.

A few moms enjoyed the luxury of working at home these days—why not fathers?

She had to admire his effort, and the fact that it couldn't be an easy proposition for him, raising two little girls alone.

Perhaps it was better not to find anything more to admire about the man, she decided, and spent the next few minutes searching for house numbers on the tree-lined block of modest brick homes. The neighborhood bespoke easy comfort and a warmth that was nurturing. A neighborhood for raising children.

Then she spotted the house number—a small ranch home with a hopscotch game drawn in white chalk on the long driveway. In the yard was a large red maple that had already begun to drop its leaves, a

signal that Denver's warm summer days were fast
drawing to an end.

Sabrina turned into the drive, carefully avoiding the
hopscotch markings, and came to a halt in front of
the double-car garage. The thought that possibly this
wasn't the best ending for the confrontation she'd had
with Gabe Lawrence yesterday afternoon assailed her.
But just as she considered backing out of the evening,
she thought of the twins and realized she very much
wanted to meet them. She just wished they didn't
have a father who rattled her senses.

When she turned off the car's engine she saw the
man in question standing at the front door. She sucked
in a breath at the sight of him. Gabe Lawrence was
every bit as intriguing as he'd been yesterday. And
just as daunting.

Those wide shoulders filled the doorway, doorjamb
to doorjamb, and she decided it was better to concen-
trate on her reason for being here: the twins and the
party she'd been invited to.

Scooping up two brightly colored birthday pack-
ages from the seat beside her, she made her way toward the front porch—and Gabe.

He greeted her with a dangerous smile, one that
made her want to reconsider her evening. "Welcome.
I thought you might have decided not to come."

Perhaps she shouldn't have.

Sabrina wondered if it was too late to plead a pre-
vious appointment. *Across town.* "Are you sure I'm
not intruding?"

"Of course not. Come on in. The party's out back."

Sabrina expected as much. She could hear the childish exuberance echoing from just that direction.

She only got a brief glimpse of the house as Gabe led her through on their way to the back patio where the party was in full swing. Sabrina dropped her carefully wrapped gifts for the twins onto a table filled with other gifts, just inside the sliding glass door in Gabe's party-cluttered kitchen.

She hadn't bought matching gifts, as most people insisted on buying for twins, but individual ones—ones she hoped each girl would enjoy.

When they reached the back, Gabe waved the two birthday girls over to meet her. He hadn't mentioned whether the twins were identical or not, but she could see now that they were—right down to their pink, little-girl party dresses and shiny new Mary Janes.

Sabrina wondered if he'd consider rereading the chapter she'd written on *that* topic in her book.

As she usually did with identicals, she tried to find some distinguishing differences so she could tell them apart, but in this case, she was at a loss. However did Gabe accomplish the feat?

She'd have to remember to ask him.

"Hi, I'm Hannah," announced one of the blond, curly-haired cherubs.

"And I'm Heather," announced the other, as if determined not to be outdone in the introductions department.

Sabrina hid a smile. "I'm pleased to meet you,

Hannah and Heather. I'm Dr. Moore—but you can call me Sabrina.''

Hannah gave an anxious glance and clung tightly to her father's pant leg. ''A...doctor? Are you gonna give us a shot?'' she voiced.

Sabrina smiled. It was something she sometimes heard from her young subjects. ''I'm a different kind of doctor, Hannah,'' she reassured the little girl. ''I don't give shots.''

''Ever?'' her twin queried.

''Ever.''

''Okay—then you can come to our party,'' Hannah allowed, as if it had become a point in question.

Sabrina smiled at them both. ''Thank you. I'd like that.''

''Tell our guest you'll talk to her later,'' Gabe interjected. ''Right now I need Sabrina's help with the hot dogs.''

The twins bounded off to rejoin their friends, and Sabrina turned to face Gabe. ''I, uh, think you got me here under false pretenses. I wasn't aware I'd have...food duty.''

He smiled. ''If you don't want to help...''

Sabrina glanced around at the children darting and dashing everywhere, whooping with exuberance, and decided food duty might not be so bad after all. She sighed. ''I'll be happy to lend a hand.''

''Great, grab an apron.''

''Who are all these children anyway?'' she asked Gabe as she snatched up the only available apron and followed him toward the grill at one end of the patio.

"Just a few neighborhood kids. Why?"

Sabrina glanced around. "No reason." She wasn't about to mention that little children made her nervous, at least outside her carefully controlled Play Lab. He'd enjoy the admission too much.

A warm evening breeze blew around the edge of the house, fragrant with the hint of pine that Sabrina always remembered from this time of year. In lieu of an apron, Gabe tucked a kitchen towel into the waistband of his lean-fitting jeans, then popped the lid on the grill.

"You man the buns and the mustard for me," he said as he deftly turned the weiners he already had cooking. "Think you can handle that?"

She was sure she could, but that hadn't been her purpose in coming. "I thought you invited me here to observe, not as slave labor," she said with just the right degree of haughtiness in her voice.

He laughed then, a deep male sound that rumbled over her senses. "I know, and I'm sorry—but I really do need some help. This is the first kid party I've ever attempted. Have a heart."

Kid parties weren't something Sabrina was all that familiar with, either, though she didn't want to relate the fact. She preferred encountering children in the clinical setting. There she was in charge. Here she felt...unsettled.

Or maybe it was being around Gabe Lawrence that had her feeling that way. "I'm surprised you didn't try something a little less...intimidating the first time. Say, one or two friends, a few paper plates, a cake."

He grinned over his shoulder at her. "What do you mean? The cake was the hardest part. Wait till you see it. Besides, this is the first real birthday I've had with the twins. And I...I wanted it to be special."

Sabrina had to admire his sentiment, the fact that he was trying so hard to put on a party for his little girls. Balloons were tethered to everything stationary, and brightly colored streamers festooned the backyard trees—all his handiwork, she was certain.

She busied herself with stuffing the hot dogs into buns and then onto plates, with a dash of mustard to round them out.

"You do a pretty fair job as assistant chef," he admitted after a while.

"Thanks—I think."

When they had the food ready, Gabe gathered up the kids and seated them at the tables he'd set up. She and Gabe settled at one end of the patio, a little apart from the group so they could at least converse over the party noise. Didn't children speak in a normal tone of voice? she wondered.

"If it's not prying too much, might I ask why this is your first birthday with the twins?" she queried. She told herself she only wanted to gain perspective about the little girls—not their all-too-sexy daddy.

Gabe kept one eye on the rowdy group, the other on the pretty woman seated across from him. The evening breeze caught the ends of her burnished brown hair, playing with the strands and setting them dancing about her face. Her eyes held a bright glint of curiosity.

He wasn't in the habit of explaining his life to people—and certainly not to women, especially ones he'd only just met—but Sabrina's question wasn't one he could easily dismiss. Though everything in him told him he should.

He shouldn't want to get to know her, or her to know him. He had a full-time job just learning to be a father to the twins. This time he intended to keep his priorities in proper perspective—and that meant not involving himself with someone as tempting as Sabrina Moore.

"Their mother and I divorced when the girls were very small," he said, deciding she could hear the truth. "Meg moved east with them—to Baltimore. I—I didn't get to see them much after that." He knew that was entirely his fault. He could have seen them, had he not been so tied up with his own busy schedule. "Six months ago Meg was killed—a car accident—and I brought the twins here to Denver to be with me."

"Gabe, I'm sorry. I—I didn't know. It must have been terrible for them."

He wasn't sure if *terrible* quite summed it up. The girls had barely known him. And they'd lost their mother, their stability. He hadn't known how to console them, and his efforts to do so had been clumsy at best.

"They've done some adjusting and they've made great strides. I'm proud of them," he said. "I'd be lying if I didn't admit there are still some rough times though. It's why I wanted to have this party for them.

I wanted them to celebrate with their new friends, and just be six years old, without all the pain they've had to get through lately.''

She didn't say a word, just moved her hand across the table to find his.

Her touch was soft and gentle. And Gabe had the feeling she could see into his soul, knew the fear he had that he might fail his daughters, understood, too, what that would do to him.

If Gabe had any idea what was good for him, he wouldn't allow Sabrina to come any closer.

Chapter Two

Gabe inserted another candle into the pink cake frosting. "I baked this myself. Not bad for a beginner, huh?"

Sabrina glanced at the caved-in center of the cake in question, then up at him. "A few more birthdays and you'll have it down pat."

"You really think so?"

She gave him a slow smile. "No, but I think it's nice that you tried. I'm sure Heather and Hannah will appreciate your efforts."

He frowned. "So it's not my best work. Check that drawer over there for a book of matches and I'll light this thing."

Sabrina slipped past him in the small kitchen and did as he asked. The man was a pushover for those two little girls, she thought. A real softy when it came

to them—and she found that an admirable trait. Not
that she had any business admiring his qualities.

She handed him the matches, and in minutes he
had the candles lit and casting a warm glow against
the pink frosting.

"Ready?" he asked, lifting the cake to carry it out
to the party.

"Ready."

"Can you handle the ice cream?"

"Almost as well as hot dog buns," she teased back.
Sabrina tried to tell herself she was not getting involved in this man's domesticity, but she wasn't so
sure she believed it.

Before, she had always been able to keep her research impersonal. Her small subjects were just that—
subjects, children she studied. She seldom involved
herself with parents—and certainly not with single
dads.

So how did she explain her presence here tonight?

Admittedly this was not her smartest move. And
she wondered if it was Gabe, or the twins, who had
been the lure.

Gabe got the birthday singing started, and by the
time he set the cake in the center of the table, the
song was in full swing, not to mention, off-key.

Sabrina tried unobtrusively to observe the twins.
The two were competitive, both with their playmates
and with each other. She suspected Gabe seldom got
a moment's peace.

Keep your focus on the siblings, not on their too-
handsome father, she reminded herself sharply.

The girls made a wish, their eyes squeezed tightly shut in determination, then blew out the candles, each trying to take center stage as they did so. Her careful research that always showed one twin as the dominant child seemed to suffer in this household. Both girls had strong personalities. Like their father?

Her thoughts got interrupted when Gabe started the assembly-line process of cake slices then ice cream. She quickly picked up the carton to scoop out the cherry-vanilla treat.

"Small amount for small child, bigger amount for big child," Gabe informed her.

She arrowed a sharp glance at him. "Thanks, but I think I can figure that out for myself."

The two little girls were eyeing her with keen anticipation. "Can I have the first piece, Dr. S'brina?"

"No, me!" begged the other twin.

Sabrina had lost track of which child was which soon after she'd arrived, something she felt badly about. Gabe could have made this easier had he not dressed the two alike.

She smiled at their rivalry. "Since you both are birthday girls, how about we do this at the same time," she said and held out a plate to each.

The two glanced at each other, then back at the plates Sabrina offered. "Okay," they chorused.

Gabe leaned toward her, his voice low, teasing. "You handled that well. If you ever decide to give up psychology, I see a brilliant future for you as a diplomat."

"Thank you, but I don't intend to give up psychology anytime soon."

No, he doubted that she would. In Gabe's opinion Sabrina Moore was a very aloof lady who believed in her research theories. He'd bet his last dollar that work came first with her.

Did she always hold her feelings in? Let anyone get close to her? What about a social life? He had to admit he was curious.

Did she kick up her heels once in a while? Or bury her nose in some boring data? Did she have a lover, a man who held her in his arms and nibbled on her neck the way he'd been tempted to do all evening?

He'd caught his gaze straying toward her more than it should, taking in her slender waist, the curve of her derriere in the skinny black skirt she wore, the creamy expanse of her throat that her green, open-necked blouse didn't hide. But what trapped his attention and held it was the shape of her pretty mouth. No woman should have a mouth like that without declaring it a lethal weapon. How could a man fight against the temptation of its slightly pouty shape? Resist its lure? He had no doubt that he'd see it in his restless sleep tonight—and probably for a few nights to come.

Gabe glanced up to see a little boy of about three peering over the edge of the table, awaiting his piece of cake. Behind him were four more kids of varying sizes. Sabrina was eyeing him, too.

"You're slowing up the show," she said, a gleam of humor in her sultry green eyes.

"Uh, sorry." He cut the little shaver an extralarge piece.

"Small kid, small amount," Sabrina whispered in rebuke.

"The kid has an appetite."

"Yeah, right." She added a scoop of ice cream to the plate Gabe handed her, a more...*manageable* scoop for the boy.

When the last child was served, and a few second helpings given out, Gabe and Sabrina got their chance to try the dessert.

"Mmm. This is good," she said, sampling a bite of the cake. "I don't even taste the sunken center."

"I wasn't aware sunken centers had a distinctive flavor," he countered.

He'd arched one eyebrow, but a smile played at his lips. For one studious moment Sabrina wondered what it would be like to feel his mouth on hers—hard, persuasive, totally distracting. Gabe was a dynamic man, one any woman would have difficulty resisting.

Herself included?

She glanced away, back to the party plate in front of her. "Actually I think it's nice you did this for your daughters," she said softly.

"Yeah, well...I hope you don't mind I roped you into this evening."

"I'll work hard to forgive you." She smiled. "Besides, I'm enjoying myself. And the twins. Very much."

His gaze swept her face. "Personally speaking or professionally?" he asked.

For a quick moment she didn't know how to answer. A blush crept up her neck. She'd just been fantasizing about the feel of his lips, their taste and what his kiss would do to her. But that was not the reason she was here. Gabe Lawrence had challenged her theories, her work…and just possibly who and what she was.

And she needed to remember that.

She lifted her chin. "Professionally," she answered.

Gabe was still considering her matter-of-fact response as the party wound down. It was still on his mind as he sent the last child home, birthday balloon and party favor in hand. The lady was keeping this evening in cool perspective.

But what about his reasons for inviting her in the first place? Had it been merely a challenge? Or a misguided desire to know more about the woman who fascinated him just a little too much? How pure had his intentions really been?

And how pure were they now?

He found Sabrina in the kitchen, her silken brown hair falling forward over one shoulder as she leaned close to the twins. Hannah held her captivated, showing her one of her birthday gifts—a new Barbie doll.

Gabe wondered what she would think about the last doll's demise.

"Sorry to break up this little discussion, but I know two girls who should be ready for dreamland."

Hannah and Heather were quick to voice their objections.

"But, Dad, we're showing Dr. S'brina what we got for our birthday," Heather announced.

"We'll go to bed later," Hannah said as if she were the one to make that decision.

Gabe hid a smile. He hated being tough on the girls, but it would take them forever to wind down after their day's excitement.

And he very much wanted to spend some time with Sabrina.

"No way," he said to his little princesses. "It's off to bed with you. Hands and faces washed, then into your pj's," he ordered. "Think you can handle that?"

Heather gave a long-suffering sigh. "*Dad*—we're not babies."

"Of course not."

He met Sabrina's gaze. She'd been observing his interplay with the twins with a keen-eyed psychologist's interest, but there was a smile on her face. For one dangerous moment he wondered how hard it would be to separate the woman from the intellectual.

He cursed the part of himself that wanted to try.

Sabrina was tempting, but she'd have to remain just that—a temptation. His little girls were his first priority these days.

"Will you stay and say g'night to us, Dr. S'brina?" Heather asked.

"Please," echoed Hannah.

Sabrina glanced down into the faces of the two little angels, then up at their handsome father. She'd stayed far too long as it was, far longer than she'd intended. *Longer* than she should.

Gabe wore a glint of a smile. Was he asking her to stay, as well?

"Say yes! Say yes!" The girls tugged on her sleeve and Sabrina laughed softly.

How could she refuse the two little look-alikes?

"Okay," she said. "I'll stay until you're ready for bed. Then I do have to go."

When the twins disappeared down the hallway, she turned to Gabe. "Want me to give you a hand with this party mess?" The kitchen could only be termed a disaster. The patio was not much better.

"Not on your life. I'll deal with the mess later. You've helped out enough this evening, considering I got you here under false pretenses."

He *had* done that, Sabrina thought. Baited her into it. "I think you made your point effectively tonight," she said quietly.

He arched a brow. "And what point is that?"

She gave a slow smile. "That possibly I don't know all there is to know about twins." At least *his* twins. "You've seemed to jump into this with both feet, theories be damned."

His eyebrow arched higher. "Is that a concession speech I hear?"

"Don't push your luck, Gabe Lawrence!"

He chuckled long and hard. "Come on, let's get away from this party mess. Care for a cold beer to wash down the taste of pink birthday punch?"

She shook her head. "Thanks, but no."

"Wine? I have a chilled bottle."

Sabrina didn't intend to stay that long. "Nothing. Thank you."

"Suit yourself."

He led her into the living room she'd glimpsed when she'd arrived. Here, at least, was relative neatness, an orderliness that was a sharp counterpoint to the chaos in his kitchen.

Sabrina turned around, taking in the room.

She read a definite male influence in the navy plaid sofa and two overstuffed chairs that looked comfy enough to sink into. A fireplace of red brick stood at the far end. She could picture Gabe here, reading a book to his daughters before a cheery blaze.

It was an image she liked.

Walking over to the mantel she picked up a framed photograph of the twins. "At the risk of hearing you hoot with laughter once again, explain to me how you tell the two apart."

To his credit he only gave one small—and short-lived—smirk. He folded his arms over his chest and came to stand next to her, so close, she could feel the heat of him, smell the clean male scent of his aftershave. This near she could see there were silver flecks that danced in the deep blue of his eyes. His mouth had a sensual fullness that tugged at her senses. She suspected his kiss would be hot, not tempered with restraint. He was a man who would demand much of a woman—*everything* from her.

He reached for the picture and their hands brushed.

His touch was warm, dangerous. "It's easy, once you know how," he said.

"Easy?"

"Hannah has a little quirk to her smile. See?" He pointed to the picture.

Sabrina studied the pose and saw what he meant.

It was a smile she'd seen before—on Gabe. She wondered if he was aware of the similarity he shared with his daughter.

"And when the twins aren't smiling, what then?" she asked.

"I try to keep this a...*happy* little family."

A hint of laughter lit his eyes. In the soft living-room light they radiated intelligence, a perception of who he was and what he wanted from life. He would command a woman's soul, as well as her heart, Sabrina thought.

The realization crossed her mind that she needed to beware.

He set the picture back on the oak mantel. "Once you get to know the twins, you'll find other differences. Hannah's laughter is bright, Heather's a little slower in coming. Hannah tilts her head to the right when she's listening to you. Heather tucks one foot behind the other when she's feeling a little...uncertain."

The two had only recently lost their mother. Yes, they would be a little hesitant, a little uncertain, Sabrina thought. But she suspected Gabe Lawrence was a good dad, though she had the feeling he didn't always consider himself to be. She felt, also, that she'd gotten a rare glimpse of the girls through their father's eyes.

Just then Hannah and Heather bounded into the room, pajamas on, faces scrubbed. One—Heather, judging by the hesitant smile—still had her hair bow in. Gabe unclipped it and tousled her hair.

Was it her professional eye that made her so aware of the relationship this small family shared with each other? For a moment she felt a pang of something akin to jealousy. Once upon a time she'd wanted this for herself. Her career, a husband, children. That was until her marriage to Phillip fell apart.

Stick with what you do best, Sabrina, she told herself.

"Will you read us a story from the new book Dad gave us for our birthday?" Heather asked.

Sabrina caught the little girl's gesture just as Gabe had described it—one foot tucked behind the other, uncertainty evident on her small, cherubic face.

Life had taught Sabrina to go slowly into relationships—or stay away from them altogether—but Gabe's twin daughters tugged at her resolve, and a few heartstrings, drawing her where she was afraid to go.

"If it's all right with your dad, just a short one," she said and glanced from Heather to her father, who was leaning a shoulder against the mantel, amusement lining his face.

He thought she couldn't do this—and he was enjoying it. His laughing eyes challenged her, much the way he'd challenged her theories yesterday afternoon.

But Sabrina intended to show him she was made of sterner stuff.

Well, what had Gabe expected!

The two little girls had taken to Sabrina like ducks to water. The woman with all the answers—or so she thought.

He paced up and down the living room, hands jammed into his pockets, feeling very much like his little experiment of the night had backfired on him, blown up in his face. He'd wanted to show the lady psychologist up for the fraud that she was. But Sabrina had been a good sport.

She'd held her own all evening. Even reading a bedtime story to his little girls.

But did she have to be so all-fired lovely in the bargain? So tempting? He was certain she would have him thumping his pillow, the vision of those sultry eyes and that wide, sensual smile of hers playing on the inside of his eyelids until the first light of day.

From the twins' bedroom he heard the lilt of her voice. Not the words, but the rhythmic cadence, occasionally her soft laugh. He had the feeling that reading to two little girls was a first for the standoffish Dr. Moore.

He'd caught her looking overwhelmed more than once during the evening. As if out of her element. Not that he couldn't feel a moment of sympathy for her. He could.

After all, this whole parent thing was still very new to him.

Which was exactly why he didn't need one pretty woman muddling his life, he thought with a groan. And he had the feeling that Sabrina Moore could do just that, given half a chance.

"Gabe."

He stopped his pacing and spun around to meet Sabrina's green-eyed gaze.

The soft light played around her face, dancing across her high cheekbones that were brushed with a faint hint of peach. Her lips glowed with the same peach hue. He stared, fascinated, as she nervously moistened them with the tip of her tongue.

Did she know how incredibly sexy that gesture was?

What it did to him?

He dragged a hand through his hair and struggled for his voice. "Don't tell me you got the twins successfully bedded down on the first try," he said, his words coming out surprisingly steady. It was more than he felt on the inside.

Sabrina smiled. "They tried to egg me into one more story, but I resisted the little charmers."

"Good," he said, taking a step closer. "I wouldn't want them to get spoiled or anything."

One soft, winged eyebrow arched attractively. "As a student of child behavior, I have to tell you it may already be too late for that, Gabe Lawrence."

He laughed.

Sabrina met his gaze. "While you're in a good mood, I have something I want to ask you," she said, her voice hesitant.

"Yeah, what's that?"

She studied his features, trying to decide how best to phrase her request.

His mouth curved up in a slow smile, his stance easy, one elbow resting against the mantel, his blue eyes probing her softly.

Sabrina drew in a steadying breath. "I would like your permission to study the girls."

"*What?*"

"Their personalities, behavior modes, adaptability to the changes in their life—"

"No!"

While she'd been explaining, Gabe's features had hardened. The sapphire of his eyes took on the color of an impending storm. In contrast, an enraged mountain lion looked tamer.

Sabrina took an instinctive step backward. "Perhaps I didn't explain well."

"On the contrary," he said. "I'm sure I understood you perfectly."

Sabrina wasn't so sure that was true. "It would be a harmless little project. The twins would do what they do naturally and I would—"

"Dissect their every action, their every word."

She blinked at his interpretation of what she did on a daily basis, her scientific methodology. "You make it sound so—"

"Cold?"

"I was going to say…disciplined."

"A softer word for the same thing," he returned, not giving an inch in his demeanor. He dragged a hand through his hair. "Those two little girls have been through a lot lately. They lost their mother," he bit out. "All they have is each other. And a single dad who's desperately trying to do the work of two parents."

"Precisely why I want to do this study," she said determinedly.

She wasn't unsympathetic to the girls' loss. Sabrina knew what the death of a parent could do to children. It was never easy to lose a mother—and her heart went out to the two little girls.

She would never do anything that would harm them or cause them pain. And she hated it that Gabe thought she might, however unintentionally.

On occasion Sabrina had had other parents refuse her—and that was their right, of course. Her research was important—but not if there was a price to pay.

She felt Gabe's gaze bore into her with the coldness of a laser beam, his shoulders squared, as if for battle.

"My work could be invaluable, a benefit both to Hannah and Heather, as well as for other children. Please tell me you'll at least think about it," she said as her final salvo.

With that she turned and started toward the front door.

"Sabrina."

She paused near the entry. She would almost think he'd reconsidered—except that she remembered the hard glint in his blue eyes and knew he hadn't changed his mind.

Still she turned around.

"I know what's best for the twins," he said flatly.

Sabrina drew in a breath. "Of course," she answered, and let herself out through the front door.

Gabe heard the decisive shut of the door and knew she was gone. He pounded on the mantel. Hannah and Heather had been doing so well, settling in here with him, making new friends. They'd begun to feel like a family together, which was what Gabe wanted for them all.

Oh, there were still times, sometimes late at night, when the twins cried for their mother, not fully understanding why she couldn't be there with them, why she couldn't hold them or kiss away their pain.

That was when Gabe would hold them, brushing away their tears, smoothing back their curls with his big ungentle hands and telling them everything would be all right, when he knew, without their mother, that would never totally be true.

Gabe went in to say good-night to his daughters and found them snuggled into the sheets on their big double bed. Their world was still too fragile for Sabrina to upset it.

But he wasn't sure she understood that.

He probably owed her some sort of apology for barking at her the way he had. Her research was important, he supposed. But Gabe just wasn't sure he dared risk two vulnerable little girls to whatever study the scientific Dr. Moore had in mind.

She'd asked him to at least consider what she'd proposed, and short of an apology, he supposed he could give her request a fair consideration.

Chapter Three

Sabrina had just returned from observing a group of four-year-old triplets in the Play Lab and she had a major headache.

"I don't want to be disturbed unless the building's on fire—and perhaps not even then," she told her secretary, Violet Franz, as Sabrina whizzed past the older woman.

Violet peered over her glasses at her. "Are you ill, child? You don't look well at all."

Alerting the motherly Violet to an illness of any magnitude would risk bringing on chicken soup—or Violet's equivalent of such.

And Sabrina didn't want that.

She needed to be alone in her office where she could forget her afternoon with the unruly triplets. The Nelson trio were adorable—*during nap time*. At play they could only be termed little hellions.

'I'm fine, Violet,'' Sabrina returned. 'I just have a lot of work to get done.''

"That may be, girl, but first you need a cup of tea,'' the woman replied.

At least it wasn't chicken soup. Sabrina would settle for tea. In truth, it sounded terrific about now. "That would be nice. Thanks.''

She ducked into her office, fully appreciating the temporary sanctuary it offered. Her desk was piled high with work in various stages of completion, and Violet had placed several phone messages neatly beside the phone. An overwatered philodendron struggled for life in front of the window, the only decoration in Sabrina's efficient, stark office.

She touched a finger to the soil in the pot, which was wet enough to grow a water lily, and wondered how she could convince Violet the poor green thing would fare much better without her constant pampering.

With a rueful smile and silent apology to the plant, Sabrina settled into her desk chair and picked up her phone messages, intent on returning the calls.

"I put a spot of lemon in,'' Violet said, interrupting Sabrina's thoughts and sashaying toward her, cup and saucer in hand. "This should fix you right up.''

Only if the tea were laced with something stronger, Sabrina thought, but she thanked Violet and accepted the cup, trying a tentative sip. It was strong and hot, the lemon a nice added flavoring. Sabrina was beginning to feel better already.

Sometimes her secretary's ministrations were helpful. "Give me a minute and I'll have my notes from the Play Lab session ready for you to type," she told Violet. "I'm feeling like a new woman alread—"

Before she could finish the sentence there was a sharp rap on the open office door. Sabrina and Violet glanced toward it in unison, but only Sabrina recognized the man filling the doorway.

Gabe Lawrence.

She gave a small gasp of surprise.

He looked totally intriguing in casual gray slacks and a crisp white shirt that hugged his lean, male torso. His hair was carelessly windblown, and a quick smile crossed his lips, then disappeared from sight. "Hope I'm not interrupting," he said. "But the door was open."

Sabrina couldn't seem to find her voice, and Violet's gaze darted from Gabe to Sabrina and back again, faster than a spectator at a tennis match. The woman was definitely curious.

And so was Sabrina.

"That's all for now, Violet," she said, not taking her eyes from the man in the doorway. "You're not interrupting a thing," she added to Gabe. "Come in."

Neither her gaze, nor Violet's, missed his easy long-legged stride as he crossed the room and settled into the chair in front of Sabrina's desk. Behind him Violet skittered out, closing the door and leaving the two of them alone.

Sabrina had not expected to see him again after the twins' birthday party two days ago, but he had never been far from her mind. She'd thought of the twins, as well. And the happy little household she'd glimpsed.

She couldn't help but wonder if Gabe had come as friend or foe. No doubt he'd read another chapter of *Multiples* to disagree with her about. She frowned.

Well, she could be big about this. "So," she said, "what brings you to the institute?"

He leaned back in his chair and drew a long breath. "I felt I owed you an apology for the other night. I hadn't meant to bark at you the way I did. And I'm sorry."

Sabrina studied his face, reading sincerity in it. "Apology accepted, though it wasn't really necessary. You're the twins' father—and it's your right to do what you feel is in their best interests."

She was just sorry that was the way he felt. Her research never hurt, it only helped.

"Yeah, well, I tend to be a little overprotective at times. Sometimes maybe too much, but I love those girls and that's why I...I'm reconsidering the project."

"The study project?" What was he saying? Sabrina tried not to get too hopeful, but she couldn't seem to help herself. It was an opportunity she wanted. She and the twins could learn from each other—and perhaps their father could learn a thing or two, as well. Though she doubted he'd ever admit to it.

He stood up and paced the room, dragging a hand through his hair. "It seems those two little girls are taken with you. *Dr. S'brina* has been all they've talked about for the past two days."

Sabrina couldn't hide a smile. It slipped out, un-bidden. "I'm pleased," she said. "They're very special little girls."

"They are. And losing their mother has been hard on them. I don't always know the...the right thing to say, the right thing to do. I try, but sometimes it comes out all wrong," he said in a not-so-easy admission. "That's why I've considered letting you work with them—if the offer still stands."

"It does." Sabrina smiled, her enthusiasm spilling out. "In fact, I can schedule the twins right away."

"Uh—about that schedule." He stilled her hand on the calendar she'd reached for.

Sabrina studied him for a moment. "I'm sure we can work out something convenient—"

"That's not what I meant. I want some control over this study."

She dropped the calendar onto her desk. "What kind of control?" she asked warily.

He sat down again. "For starters, I don't want the research done here in this place. It's too—" he glanced around at her severe office setting, the blue-gray walls dotted with her lofty diplomas "—ster-ile," he finished.

Sabrina suddenly saw the room through his eyes. She was always working on a new project, never having the time to give the space...a feminine touch. Maybe she'd add a few pictures, some more plants, change the wall coloring. When she found that elusive time, that was.

She returned her gaze to him. "This office suits my

purposes," she said. "But I wouldn't be doing the study here. Rather it would be in the Play Lab. I can assure you it's bright and cheer—"

"No!"

"No?"

"I won't have the twins studied at any stuffy institute."

"And where do you suggest?"

"Kid places—the park, the playground. Saturday I'm taking the twins hiking in the woods. The outdoors is the perfect spot to begin. That is, if you want to come along."

Wherever the twins are, Gabe wouldn't be far away—and considering the way the man affected her, that was a danger she didn't need. Sabrina should tell him no right now and be done with it—but something in her couldn't say the words.

His eyes were steeled on her, awaiting her answer. She felt their pull, their tug, reaching that part of her she'd vowed to keep out of harm's way. She didn't need her emotions tied in an unravelable knot while trying to do her study. Still, this was an opportunity she wasn't sure she wanted to pass up.

If those two little kids came with a father attached, she'd work through it somehow.

"Saturday. A hike in the woods. Sounds like a perfect place to begin," she said, though she couldn't imagine anything further from the truth.

Sabrina arrived Saturday morning on time and looking sexier than any lady psychologist had a right to look, Gabe thought, as he and the twins greeted her at the door. His welcome was restrained, the twins' boisterous as they proudly showed off their new hiking gear to her. Gabe was busier taking in the fit of *Sabrina's* hiking gear, from the sweatband around her silky hair pulled into a bouncy ponytail, to the shape of her small firm breasts beneath her plum-colored T-shirt that teased at his imagination, to the taut fit of her jeans tucked into neat hiking boots.

"You look like you could tackle Mount Everest in those boots," he said when she caught his gaze slithering up and down her cute shape.

"I hope you don't have anything that energetic in mind. I know two little girls who might find it a bit much. Not to mention one big girl."

Climbing Mount Everest was *not* what he'd like to do with her—but that was something best left unconsidered. Sabrina was here to work with the twins—nothing more, he reminded himself. And he was just along for the ride.

"Well, let's get going," he said and ushered the troops out the door and into the family 4×4.

He checked the twins' seat belts, certain they were properly hooked and adjusted, then turned to Sabrina.

"I'm sure I can buckle my own," she said with a wry smile, then set out to prove it.

"It's just this father thing," he said. "Stop me if I try to tie your shoelaces or wipe your runny nose—okay?"

"I'll try to remember," she returned. "But you

know, it wouldn't hurt to let the girls do a few things for themselves.''

That was the psychologist in her talking. He frowned. ''Hey, I take this daddy business seriously.''

Soon they were off, headed down the highway west toward the mountains and his favorite place to hike. If they followed the lower trail, the incline wouldn't be too steep for a pair of six-year-olds. He also didn't want to wear Sabrina out on their first outing. She was being a good sport, agreeing to his conditions for this study project.

He knew she'd wanted—*expected*—to do her work within the confines of her hallowed institute, but his way was better for the twins. However, considering how enticing Sabrina looked today, he would have hell to pay for his insistence.

The woman had done nothing but bring him grief, even before he'd met her, he realized. From the moment he'd first cracked open her book and read her theories on parenting twins. But he wouldn't allow his little look-alikes to be put into any stuffy category, become some scientific statistic. Life was real, parenting was real. *Very real,* he'd found out. And he figured it was about time Sabrina found out about it, too.

''Anyone for singing?'' he tossed out to the group at large. He was determined to keep this day fun.

The twins quickly chorused a ''yes'' and launched into a kiddie tune Gabe didn't know the words to. Neither did Sabrina, but he caught her listening to the lyrics and she joined in on the chorus.

"You're not singing," she chastised after the third verse of the tune.

He smiled. "I'm enjoying the concert."

They reached the start of the trail and Gabe parked the car under a tree.

"I wanna walk with S'brina," Hannah stated.

"No, me," chimed Heather.

Gabe gave a low groan at the sibling rivalry he hadn't yet learned how to corral, then turned to Sabrina and gave her a nonverbal go-ahead to field this one.

"How about we take turns?" she placated.

Gabe knew that one never worked. He'd tried it before.

He picked up his backpack, stuffed with picnic goodies for a little repast at the halfway point, as Sabrina suggested Hannah be the first to walk with her since she'd asked first.

Gabe gave a slow smile and waited for that little idea to backfire, but to his surprise, it didn't. Heather acquiesced to wait her turn as Sabrina suggested.

What potent magic did the woman possess? he wondered warily. He'd have to ask her.

He handed her a second backpack, containing a few first-aid items he hoped no one would need, some bottled water for the hike and a few nutrition bars for quick energy. "Are we ready to hit the trail?" he asked.

"Ready," answered the group.

He reached for Heather's hand and she slipped it easily into his larger one. It was a gesture that never

failed to remind him that he'd missed out on so much
of the girls' younger years, years he could never get
back. They were gone forever. But today was not.
Today they could build new memories, like the birthday party the other day. And there would be more,
new ones to share.

Gabe felt better about the day, even about having
Sabrina along. She just might be good for the girls, a
feminine influence in their young lives. The two had
taken to her like bees to a sunflower. He only wished
he hadn't made the same fast trip.

He took the lead and pointed out things of interest
along the path. He had the girls stop and listen to the
chatter of the aspen leaves, observe the brilliant scar-
let plumage on an oriole that ventured close. He also
picked a wildflower and handed it to Sabrina.

She hesitated a moment before taking it, then a soft
smile bloomed on her pretty lips. "Are you always
this gallant when you go hiking in the woods?" she
asked, feigning a disbelief at his gesture.

He wished he knew what it was about Sabrina that
made him act like a goofy twelve-year-old. "Maybe
you just…inspire me."

She seemed to doubt that, but she sniffed the yel-
low blossom, then tucked it into the sweatband
around her head, where it bobbed and waved like an
Indian feather. The twins, not wanting to be left out
of anything, requested a flower, too, so Gabe spent
the next few minutes searching along the trail for just
the right one for each.

The girls tired more quickly than he'd expected, so

at the first clearing they came to, they stopped for lunch.

"Why is it everything tastes better out-of-doors?" Sabrina asked when they'd spread out the contents of Gabe's backpack, adding a few things from hers, as well.

Gabe had thought of everything, she realized, right down to the red-and-white paper tablecloth, which they'd strewn over the grass at the edge of the woods.

"All we need are a few picnic ants," he returned, to which the twins added a repugnant *"Gross!"*

Their father grinned. "Definitely city girls," he bantered to Sabrina.

"You can count me in that category, too, I'm afraid," she admitted.

"I'm hiking with a whole *group* of wusses?"

The twins giggled and Sabrina draped an arm around each child. "We are not wusses, are we, girls?"

"No," they chorused, and all three fixed the man with a fierce glower.

"Take it back, Dad," Hannah said.

"Yeah," chimed Sabrina and Heather.

He threw his hands up in mock surrender. "I know when I'm outnumbered. You are not wusses. There— is that better?"

The three looked at each other. "Shall we forgive him?" Sabrina asked her two small cohorts.

The girls decided to let him off the hook, but they had conditions. "If he takes us to play min'ture golf," Heather said.

"And buys us ice cream," added Hannah.

He glanced at each twin, then at Sabrina. "Well—what's your demand?" he asked her.

She would settle for a kiss, Sabrina decided. A soft brush of his lips against hers. He looked so all-fired sexy today in khaki safari shorts and a faded navy sweatshirt that fit him like a second skin. And his grin was enticing, naughty.

"I, uh, think I'll take a rain check on my demand," she answered.

His naughty grin widened, as if he'd read her mind, and Sabrina felt a slow, but intense blush creep onto her cheeks. This outing was to be a chance to get to know the twins better, do research—but that wasn't the way the day was turning out. She'd done zilch on research and a whole lot of laughing with the girls, sharing with them and...ganging up on their father—the latter also enjoyable—all in fun of course.

Fun. When had that word crept into her vocabulary? And should she allow it to stay? Having fun was good in and of itself, but distracting, definitely distracting, to her goals.

Phillip had accused her of being a cold fish, her nose always buried in the latest set of statistics. But emotions could hurt, Sabrina had learned. And emotions could get in the way of research that needed to remain...dispassionate.

The four ate their picnic lunch, then searched for four-leaf clovers in the grass. The twins tired of the quest after a short while and made a clover chain out of the flowers.

"This is for S'brina," they said proudly when it reached an appropriate length. S'brina, not *Dr.* S'brina. No children in her studies had ever dropped the doctor part of her name....

And *none* had ever, ever, made her a delicate chain to wear around her neck.

She brushed her fingers over the blossoms, her heart lodged somewhere in her throat, and glanced down at their smiling faces. How innocent children were, how free with their emotions. She wished she knew how to be that free, how to trust that innocently, how to love without worrying about whether that love would be returned, or last.

Maybe there were a few things she could learn from Hannah and Heather. The thought frightened Sabrina to death.

"Th-thank you," she managed to say to the girls.

"If you don't break the chain you get your favoritest wish," Hannah explained.

"That's not true," Heather told her sister. "You made that up."

"So..." her twin returned, "what's wrong with that?"

What was wrong with it indeed? Sabrina thought. Was it so wrong to want a little magic in your life, to make a wish—and have it come true? "I think that's a lovely belief, Hannah," she told her. "And if you want to make it up, it's okay."

But Sabrina couldn't decide what her favorite wish might be—she hadn't had a lot of practice at it. She dealt with reality. And that was something she had to remember. Wishes were for little girls—and she'd left her childhood behind a long time ago. If she'd ever had one. She'd always been a serious child, playing alone, *left* alone much of the time because her parents had been so preoccupied with their own pursuits, their own accomplishments.

She glanced at Gabe who'd been observing this exchange with the twins intently. What was he thinking? she wondered.

And why did he have such an enigmatic smile on his face?

Chapter Four

Gabe gathered up the remainder of their picnic lunch, depositing the trash in a receptacle positioned near the trail. Sabrina had requested some time alone with Heather and Hannah. She wanted to administer a few skill tests to them, tests to determine each child's dominant and lesser attributes.

It all sounded ridiculous to Gabe. He knew his kids backward and forward by now, and he could *give* her the facts she needed—had she asked. Hannah was the bossy one, acting a little too big for her britches sometimes. Heather was the peacemaker in their little family. Hannah was a ham, Heather a little more hesitant.

Sabrina also wanted to know which twin had been born first, and Hannah had clearly let her know *she* was the oldest. By four minutes. Though Gabe couldn't see what kind of difference it made—beyond the fact that his sweet little Hannah loved to rub it in to her sister.

But if Sabrina wanted time alone with them, he would oblige her. Besides, he wanted to explore the area. He returned from depositing the trash to find the three of them seated in a semicircle, Sabrina between them. The sun glinted off her silky brown hair, striking it with rich strands of spun gold.

What did this woman really know about twins that he hadn't already learned—the hard way? Could two little girls who bore the same genetics be reduced to scientific terms? His babies were real kids—bright and clever, sweet and ornery. And a whole lot lovable.

Sabrina glanced up as he neared. "Did you want something?" she asked.

Oh, yes, he wanted. He wanted to get beneath this woman's bookish facade, prove to her that statistics were dull and boring and that—bottom line—it was what was in a person's heart that mattered. Not the way they fit onto some graph or into a learning curve.

But he suspected Sabrina never got that close to her subjects, *never let them get that close to her*. He also suspected that if Sabrina stuck around long enough, Hannah and Heather would change that. He doubted even she could resist his little charmers.

They certainly had *Gabe* wrapped around their six-year-old pinkies.

"Not a thing," he said. "I'm off to explore that brook over there. How long do you think this—" he waved a hand at her silly study sheets "—will take?"

"Not long at all. Children have a short attention span, as you probably know. I just want to do some preliminary stuff, and then we'll join you. Okay?"

Silver flecks swam in her eyes and her lips held a succulent secret he wanted to taste. He'd leave her to her busywork, sit beside the stream and count the trout swim by—if there were any that pollution hadn't yet destroyed. He'd try to forget the image of this woman that had tripped through his mind with increasing regularity ever since he'd met her.

"Sure," he said. "Hannah, Heather, you do what Dr. Sabrina tells you."

She was *Dr.* Sabrina again. She'd put on the Ph.D. hat that had begun to slip just a little earlier. About the time she'd begun to seem...human.

That was the Sabrina that appealed to him, that shook his timbers. It was also the Sabrina he should stay away from—though he doubted half a world away would be distance enough.

He blew his two cherubs a kiss, which made them giggle, then he left the trio alone.

Sabrina watched the big man saunter away. He'd gone—but not far enough to give her senses a break. His tree-trunk-hard body still remained within her range of vision, the clean mossy scent of him lingered to taunt her.

He smiled and waved—and Sabrina knew it wasn't the twins' attention span she should be worried about, but her own.

"Are you gonna test us now?" Hannah asked, drawing Sabrina back to her intentions.

A guilty flush crept up her neck, as if the two little pixies knew her mind had strayed—and to where. "This is never going to work," she said aloud.

Two sets of big blue eyes peered up at her through thick lashes. "Did—did we do something wrong?" Heather voiced softly.

Sabrina gave them each a reassuring smile. "Oh, no, darlings, not you. It's—" Their *father,* she thought silently. And just possibly herself. Yes, herself, for ever agreeing to his demands. "It's just that I usually work in my Play Lab, not out here alongside—" She glanced over at Gabe, sitting on the grassy bank, his back to a tall oak. He was gazing up at the sky as if he didn't have a care in the world. "Nature," she finished.

"Do kids get ta play in your Play Lab?" Hannah wanted to know.

"And can *we* play there?" Heather asked.

Sabrina brushed a hand over their blond curls. "Maybe one day I'll show it to you, but right now we're going to work—uh, *play* here."

She'd agreed to Gabe's rules regarding his daughters, and now she would have to abide by them.

For the next thirty minutes Sabrina ran the two girls through the cursory evaluation sheets she'd brought with her. She'd designed these tests herself and made them fun for the young children she studied by letting them complete them using brightly colored crayons.

At the end of the session she collected the pages. She'd digest them in better detail later, but her offhand glance now told her these two little look-alikes were bright and clever kids, adaptable to changes in their lives and patently curious. They had very loving natures and a warmth that ran deep. For a moment Sabrina wondered just how much of this she'd gleaned from the tests and how much from the girls themselves. But that, she knew, was unscientific and could bias her raw data.

It was better to keep the twins at arm's length. The way she did all the children. But she suspected with Hannah and Heather that would be difficult—and just possibly she would end up the loser for it.

Better that than risk her heart, risk emotions best kept under lock and key, emotions that could devastate her when she had to walk away, out of their lives.

She'd had to walk away before—from her marriage, from hopes and dreams, everything she thought she'd once wanted. She couldn't risk that again.

At the institute she was safe and secure from that frightening, big world out there. It was where she belonged, her heart tethered to her studies, her research.

The twins helped Sabrina gather up the crayons, which she placed in her knapsack along with the work pages they'd completed, and then she slung the bag over her shoulder.

"Ready for the rest of that hike?" she asked them.

The girls chorused that they were, then bounded spiritedly over to their dad, who swept first one twin, then the other, up in his big arms, arms that would make little girls feel secure, Sabrina knew. Arms that would make a *woman* feel secure—in a way that little else could.

"So, how did the session go?" he asked, setting the two down again.

They scampered over to observe a bird nest that had fallen from a tall red maple, and Sabrina smiled at their curiosity. This was a wonderful age group to study, one that never failed to intrigue her.

She only wished their father didn't intrigue her, as well.

"The session went fine. But…"

How could she tell him he kept her slightly off balance? That he rattled her senses just a little too much?

"But…?" he repeated. "Is there a problem?"

Only that he was standing too close for her to think clearly, too close for her to explain that she needed her space—a healthier distance from him and his two little darlings.

She needed to maintain her perspective, and the Play Lab would enable her to do that. It was her safe haven, where fathers of twins didn't tempt her senses, didn't remind her she was a woman—a woman with needs, wants, emotions that at the moment were a tad too shaky.

"I'm just having some trouble adapting to this less-than-scientific environment," she said. And the man who made her just a little crazy.

"Ah…as in that stuffy institute of yours. We had a deal, Sabrina."

Yes, they had a deal—that she would study his children on their own turf. She just hadn't realized how difficult it could make her life, how much one handsome hunk of a father could tempt her senses. But she'd agreed to his deal—and she wouldn't be the one to break the arrangement.

The twins had been through a lot lately, losing their mother. And if she could help, in whatever small way, she wanted to. She also wanted to get to know them better, spend time with them. For themselves. For herself.

And their troublesome father? What about him?

She shoved that thought away, unanswered. "If you'd only stop in and see the Play Lab, you'd find it's not the stuffy place you seem to think it is," she explained.

Gabe considered the point. He didn't know about Play Labs. And he didn't know what it was about the woman in front of him that had him so bothered, *sensually* bothered.

She smelled sweet, like honeysuckle drowsing in the early-morning sun. Her scent teased at him, making him want what he shouldn't have. "Maybe one day I'll come by and…investigate this lab of yours," he said.

He fought the urge to touch her cheek—and lost. She didn't draw away, but instead swayed forward slightly as if his touch was dizzying somehow. Her skin was soft, silky, beneath the rasp of his fingertips. He longed to trail them over every inch of her, watch her eyes widen, flare with heat, the way they were doing now, a reflex she couldn't control any more than he could his own actions.

"Gabe, I think—"

He silenced her with a touch of his finger to her lips. "I'd say you think too much. Don't you ever let loose, have fun?"

He wished she'd have fun with him. He liked her, her sweetness, her beauty, the shape of her, even that fine mind she'd paraded off in her book. But he wanted to reach the woman beneath that mind, the woman who kept herself aloof—as if she'd somehow been hurt before. A woman who thought it safer to retreat into charts and graphs and writing stuffy research books about kids she never tried to reach.

That wouldn't happen with his kids. Not if he could help it.

"Why don't we compromise?" he said, brushing her lower lip, wanting very much to taste its pouty fullness. "I'll give you whatever time alone you need with the twins—your own space. I'll make myself scarce—if that's what you want, Sabrina."

His touch was seductive. His voice even more so. Scarce wasn't at all what Sabrina wanted at the moment. The brush of his fingertips held her spellbound, too mesmerized to think about Play Labs or research projects. Instead, she imagined what emotions he might unleash in her if his mouth followed where his finger had been.

Right now he made her a little insane, a little crazy.

She wanted him to kiss her. Wanted it for no sane reason. Wanted it, knowing it could only complicate the already-difficult relationship she had with him, impair her judgment, her work with the twins and everything she held dear.

"You're tempting, Sabrina, very tempting," his voice rasped. He leaned in closer, his lips only a warm breath away. Her eyes whispered shut as she anticipated his kiss, the taste of him.

A kiss that didn't happen.

Two noisy little girls intruded on the quiet moment, exclaiming they'd found a baby bird and that the adults had to come and see.

Sabrina should have felt relief—there was no way she could have kept a kiss from this man in any proper perspective. Instead, what she felt bore the sharp taste of regret.

"Who wants ice cream?" Gabe asked when they'd left the horizon of mountains far behind and slipped into Denver's heavy suburban traffic.

He wished he could leave his want behind as easily. Had it not been for his pair of six-year-olds, he'd have blundered into a kiss with a woman who heated his insides to a degree that rivaled hell. On a hot day.

What had he been thinking of? He had a second chance to make things right in his life, a second chance with his kids few men ever got—the chance to be their dad, this time in a meaningful way.

He hated it that Meg had died, that she would never see the twins grow up. But because of that cruel twist of fate that had caused Meg her life, he had the opportunity to be a *real* father, a caring one.

So why did he want to go and complicate things by falling for a woman he needed like he needed a bad cold?

Maybe a bad cold was too tame. Try major root canal, he thought again.

"Me! Me!" shouted the twins from the back seat.

"And what about you?" he asked Sabrina, giving her a smile.

For a moment Sabrina didn't know what to say. She'd almost kissed this man back there on the trail. Worse, she'd wanted it. She should leave well enough alone, bow out of any trip for ice cream.

She would have other opportunities with the twins—perhaps when she had her head screwed on a little straighter regarding their father, she thought.

"Uh, count me out. I...really should get home. If you'd drop me at your place, I'll get my car and—"

"Come, too, S'brina," Hannah said.

"We want S'brina," added her sister.

"You'll disappoint the twins," Gabe said, not playing fair at all. "What do you have to do at home that can't wait? A rough trek through the woods calls for an ice-cream sundae," he explained.

He really wasn't playing fair.

Sabrina was beginning to feel trapped. By Gabe. By the twins' pleas that touched a chord in her—one the little sweethearts had been thrumming on long and hard since she'd met them. She smiled at the twins. "I'd think ice cream would be the treat here, not having *me* tag along."

"Oh—I think you're very much the attraction," Gabe added in a way that made her heart trip over an errant beat.

She searched around for her willpower. Everything

in her told her she'd only complicate the day more by giving in. She turned to the twins to offer an excuse, to beg off until another time, but the words wouldn't come.

In truth, she didn't really want to spend her evening at home, absorbed in boring research data. She'd rather watch the two enjoy ice cream, their little cheeks smeared with chocolate or tutti-frutti. And Gabe? her conscience pricked. What about him?

Did she want to enjoy *his* company, as well?

She warred with that question a short minute more, then caved in, hating herself for doing so.

"Okay," she said. "Maybe one quick sundae."

"Yeah!" chorused the twins.

Ten minutes later they trooped into the Dairy Cone, Gabe leading the way, Sabrina bringing up the rear. While Gabe placed their order, Sabrina collected the two little girls and attempted to herd them into a small corner booth.

"See that big drippy cone over there?" Heather asked when they were seated.

Sabrina glanced up at the store's giant logo that Heather had pointed to. "What about it?" she asked.

"Our dad made it," she said.

"*D'zigned* it," Hannah corrected, in a superior-sister attitude.

Sabrina hid a smile at the two, but she was curious about the girls' remark. The store had opened recently to great popularity and two more stores had sprouted up faster than weeds after a rain. Was this logo really Gabe's handiwork?

Just then, he sauntered toward them, carrying a tray loaded with ice-cream boats, the large ones presumably for Sabrina and him, the smaller versions for the twins, all looking sinfully delicious. "Is it true?" she asked him.

"Is what true?" He set the tray down on the table and began handing out ice cream to each of them, along with rose-colored plastic spoons and an ample supply of napkins.

She hooked a thumb at the giant logo hanging prominently behind the soda fountain and duplicated on all the store's advertising.

"Ah, that. The girls have been bragging about their dad again." He tweaked their noses playfully. "Yes, that's one of my endeavors."

"And we get free ice cream whenever we want," Hannah added gleefully.

Gabe grinned. "A small perk the girls seem to think is terrific. They also think they should take advantage of it daily." He patted his waist. "To their father's downfall."

The ice cream must not contain too many calories per scoop, judging by Gabe's hard lean body, Sabrina decided, though she kept the thought to herself. "Well, I, for one, am impressed," she told him.

"It was a lucrative account for me, one that enabled me to sit back and take it easy jobwise for a while. And get to know my kids," he added.

He said it like that was what mattered most in his life—not the money, nor the *plum* account, but one little pair of twins.

The girls begged to go check out the ice-cream case to see if the store had added any new flavors or toppings—like peppermint sprinkles. Gabe gave them permission, but told them not to bother Maxine behind the counter.

"You're very good with them," she said quietly when they'd traipsed off.

He glanced up, and his deep blue gaze studied her for a long moment. "I'm not so sure of that," he said finally. "According to a few of your theories, Doctor, I'm doing *everything* wrong."

"Perhaps not as wrong as you might think."

Sabrina was beginning to see the human factor at work in the art of raising twins. Maybe, just maybe, her insistent, by-the-book approach wasn't the only way to look at child rearing. There was a lot to be said for the seat-of-the-pants method of raising kids, as well. Gabe was proof of that.

He stirred in a little caring, a little tenderness and a whole lot of love—emotions that reached a child, no matter how many mistakes a parent made along the way.

He arched an eyebrow at her about-face. "Did I hear you correctly, Doctor? Are you saying your preaching may not be all it's cracked up to be?"

The man couldn't quit while he was ahead. He had to go and ruffle her feathers. "I'm only saying that you're not doing such a bad job of looking after the twins," she returned. "Don't push it further or I'll take it back."

He laughed then, long and heartily, and Sabrina

liked the sound of it. "Seriously—it can't be easy raising two little girls alone," she said. "Care to let me in on just how you do it?"

He'd aroused her scientific curiosity. She might just want to add the single-father aspect to her next book, she told herself. That was, if she could learn to deal with Gabe Lawrence on some level beside the *physical.*

"Seriously, huh?" He leaned back in the booth, looking nothing at all like a Mr. Mom.

Sabrina worked to dismiss his potent male image from her mind, to corral her wild thoughts. "I'm interested," she said.

So was Gabe, though more in the woman seated across from him than in the conversation. "Fathers don't exactly come equipped with the nurturing gene, and twins don't come with an instruction manual, either. In the beginning I made a few mistakes. I still do."

"The twins don't seem to suffer from it."

He lifted an eyebrow. "Did you learn that from those dubious tests of yours, Doctor?" he asked her.

"No. From observation."

Gabe squirmed. More than once he'd felt the heat of her gaze on him. He had hoped it was feminine interest, but apparently it had been…cold analysis. Did the woman ever have a thought that wasn't related to her work? He'd love to shake her loose from it—just once. To watch her lose control.

"Your scientific study extends to me, as well, then," he said.

She arched a brow. "Only in regard to the way you interact with the twins, I'm afraid. As a parent of multiples, a single parent—*male* single parent—you *are* a rarity."

He frowned. "You make me sound like some sort of unusual microbe you'd like to probe."

She had the good grace to look embarrassed at that. In fact, he sort of enjoyed watching the blush climb up her pretty neck and decorate her cheekbones. Her green eyes blinked behind thick lashes, and it took her a moment to raise her gaze to meet his again. "I'm sorry. I know I have a habit of taking my work a little too seriously sometimes. All I meant was—"

"That you take your work a little too seriously," he repeated. He wasn't letting her off with any easy explanation. Not when it was a fact.

Once, he had done the same—and it had cost him a marriage, his family and the early years of watching the twins grow, years he could never get back. Sometimes you had to look at the world in a different way. But he wasn't sure Sabrina knew that. And that was a shame. She had a beautiful warm side to her, but one he suspected she rarely unleashed.

Sabrina studied her ice cream. Under Gabe's intent gaze she felt like she was the one being probed. So it was a flaw of hers—one she wasn't sure was so wrong. Her work defined her; it was who Dr. Sabrina Moore was, what she was about.

Phillip had said she hid behind her work, used it as an excuse to avoid relating to him, to others. The truth was it had always been hard for her to open up, lay out her feelings for others to see. She'd thought she was learning how with Phillip. But he'd found someone else, someone he'd said he loved. He'd taken her exposed feelings and trampled them before they'd gotten the chance to bloom.

She'd learned how fragile feelings were, how easily bruised—and she wasn't at all sure she wanted to trot them out again.

In her work, feelings only got in the way of facts, confused carefully thought-out equations. In relationships, she'd learned, they did the same. At least for her.

She envied Gabe his family, the love she'd seen at work in their home. She envied him the security to place his daughters first in his life, ahead of his own fulfillment, both jobwise and perhaps even relationshipwise.

She envied him his twins, two sweet little girls he'd taken to his heart, unselfishly giving them what they needed most: himself.

"Just how did we get this conversation turned around? I believe we were discussing you," she said. She pushed her nearly empty ice-cream boat away, followed by her napkin. "Tell me about your ad agency. How long have you been creating logos— like giant ice cream cones?"

So, they were back to him again. Gabe would have preferred to talk about Sabrina. He wanted to know what had caused that soft, sad smile to play at her lips. Why she looked so fragile right now, so vulnerable.

But he doubted Sabrina was going to tell him. "Actually...I lucked into that account. The company was looking for someone local who could handle the advertising for their new store concept. They didn't want the Madison Avenue boys, so I bagged their business by being Denver-based."

"Have you been in advertising long?" she asked, her eyes soft and warm.

"Long enough. I'll show you a few billboards on the way back that were my brainchild. The twins get a kick out of seeing Dad's work go up on those big road signs."

"And in ice-cream parlors," she added with a grin.

He smiled. "Yeah, especially in ice-cream parlors."

"It sounds like a lot of work, starting an ad agency and keeping it going."

"I put in a lot of hours in the beginning—to the detriment of my young family, as it turned out...."

"Your divorce?" she asked at his silence.

He nodded. "Back then I was trying to put my little agency on the map, so to speak."

"And now?"

He paused again. "I don't do anything without the twins in mind. I refuse to take on more than I can handle."

"You're lucky to be able to work at home."

He smiled. "I try to remember that when the girls are fighting over the red crayon, the washing machine spews out soapsuds because Hannah tried to wash her Barbie clothes with half a box of detergent and

Heather won't let the answering machine pick up the calls, telling whoever is on the line that 'Dad is right here.'"

"Maybe you really are a Mr. Mom."

"What?"

Sabrina hadn't realized she'd spoken aloud. She smiled. "Nothing."

Just then Hannah and Heather returned to inform them that the place had forty flavors of ice cream.

"We counted 'em."

"All of 'em."

"Can we come back tomorrow, Dad? And can S'brina come, too?"

Something warm lodged in Sabrina's heart. She felt included in this little family, however briefly. And although she knew that should frighten her to death, it didn't.

At least she *told* herself it didn't.

Chapter Five

"I guess we should set a date for your next meeting with the twins. I'll leave it up to you as to when and where—as long as you stick by our agreement," Gabe said.

"That leaves the park, your place, the zoo...."

"The pizza shop, miniature golf...take your pick," Gabe returned.

Name her poison. Sabrina knew anything she chose would involve her casually with the twins, and with Gabe. And she'd have to be a hard-hearted woman to be able to resist the little darlings.

And their father?

She needed a little hard-heartedness where he was concerned. Definitely.

"I have several talks scheduled for next week and another book signing for *Multiples,* so I really won't be free until Friday."

"Busy schedule, lady."

Yes, she was busy, and remaining that way just might take her mind off the man who intrigued her just a little too much. She needed some space from Gabe, his two small cherubs and these crazy stirrings she'd never experienced with such intensity before, and which she wasn't at all certain how to explain.

The best thing to do was to get her mind back on her research, her energies carefully channeled in the same direction.

"Why don't I call you toward the end of the week?" he suggested.

"That would be fine," she said.

They'd reached Gabe's place and her car was parked in the driveway. Her day with the twins, with *Gabe,* was at an end. She smiled at the girls and told them she'd see them again soon, but before she could get out the words, they reached up to wrap their small arms around her neck. It gave her a wonderful, warm feeling she'd never expected, and she returned their hugs.

Confused by the mixture of new emotions the day had evoked in her, she said a quick goodbye, then slipped behind the wheel of her car and escaped out of the driveway. Still, she expected that thoughts of the day she'd spent, the near-kiss with Gabe on the mountain trail and the girls' spontaneous little hugs would keep her unfocused for several confusing days to come.

It was the final talk of Sabrina's week and she felt a small edge of relief that she could finally get back to what she did best: research. Still, she had enjoyed this teaching stint and the promotion of her book, *Multiples*.

Tonight's group of moms had listened eagerly, then asked questions, intelligent ones, ones that kept her on her toes—and her mind from straying to the *non*-mom in the third row.

Gabe Lawrence had been the last person she'd expected to see here tonight. Although she tamped down her excitement that he was here, her glance had continued to wander toward him, skimming over his wide shoulders, and the hint of the five o'clock shadow that graced his lean, square jaw.

When their eyes met, she thought she would drown in the blueness of his gaze. She felt its heat, its lure to surrender some part of herself to him. But that was not something she intended to do. Especially not with this man, who made her feel too much like a woman—and even less like a scientist.

When the class ended, he made his way to the front of the room. Sabrina watched as he excused himself to a few moms standing in the aisle as he edged around them. She didn't miss the admiring glances they gave him, or the half-envious ones when he stopped to speak to her. The man was too much for any woman's senses.

Hers included.

Gabe gave her a tilted smile that set her heart to fluttering. "Care to go somewhere for coffee and a little conversation?" he asked.

Offhand, Sabrina could think of half a dozen reasons she shouldn't, all of them having to do with this man's charm and male good looks. "I have to sign a few books for the mothers," she said, hoping the line of women waiting to speak to her would stretch out the door, and that Gabe wouldn't want to wait.

"No hurry," he said. "I'll be right over there when you're done." He pointed to a spot by the door.

Well, she'd gotten herself into this when she asked if she could include Hannah and Heather in her study. Now there was a price to be paid.

A *handsome* price, she thought, tearing her gaze away from his easy nonchalance as he leaned back against the wall, smiling at the ladies around him.

They did their share of looking, too, though Sabrina wasn't sure she could blame them.

When the line in front of her finally dwindled and the last mother trekked from the room, she realized she was alone—with Gabe. He sauntered over to where she stood gathering up her things.

"How did you know where to find me?" she asked, more than a little curious. She hadn't remembered telling him where she'd be, only that she was busy this week giving talks, signing books.

"Your secretary was very informative."

Violet. Sabrina sighed.

The woman had quizzed her all week about Gabe, keeping him at the forefront of her mind when Sabrina would have preferred banishing him from it.

The twins, too, had been in her thoughts—the day

she'd spent with them, the clover chain they'd made for her...their earnest little hugs.

The man—and his little charmers—had been a definite distraction.

"Gabe, I..."

"I know—you're going to tell me you're A) Too busy, B) Too tired, C) Have work to do or D)—"

"Accept."

"Accept?"

She did need to set a time with him for her next session with the twins, though a phone call could have accomplished the same purpose. But he was here. And she could use the pick-me-up. "As long as it's an early night. I have—" she laughed "—a lot of work to do."

"You're a woman with a lot of excuses."

"Or maybe just a busy one?" she proffered.

"Maybe."

The coffee bar Gabe chose was cozy, with small tables for two—three, if forced into an add-on—and definitely intimate. Sabrina would have to work to keep things casual between them. This was not a date, no matter how much it was beginning to feel like one.

She ordered an amaretto-flavored coffee and took her drink to the best-lit table in the little bar, though it was still only slightly brighter than a cave at midnight, she decided.

Gabe ordered an ice coffee and joined her at the table. "You had a good group tonight," he said, offering her an all-too-sexy smile.

She played with her napkin, intent on dispelling the

impact of this man on her senses. "Yes, it was a good group. I—I was surprised to see you there. Did you come to learn a few things—or to object to another one of my careful theories?"

He tried to subdue her gaze with his own—and did a pretty fair job of it. "I came to see *you*." He grinned. "It's not often I can find a sitter and get a night out."

His eyes were hypnotic, his words dangerous, her feelings equally dangerous, threatening all her good sense.

"And how did you manage *this* night out? I mean, without the twins in tow?"

Keep this casual, she reminded herself. This was just a case of Mr. Mom syndrome, something she could learn from for that chapter in her next book. Gabe was a single dad—and how better to learn, than to observe one in action.

He smiled. "I, uh, traded babysitting services with one of the neighborhood mothers. Sue Chandler takes the twins tonight; I entertain her toddler on Saturday."

She was right. She could learn volumes for her research. "Sounds like a terrific arrangement." It couldn't be easy for a man trying to raise his daughters alone. And Gabe was doing it so admirably.

Without her learned advice.

That last thought irritated—more than she cared to admit.

Gabe gazed at her across the table. The twins had spent the better part of the week talking about Dr.

S'brina. He'd been having a difficult time as it was, keeping the woman off his mind.

Seeing her now, he was certain his coming here tonight was not the move of a sane man. She looked so delectable, a pair of glasses perched on the end of her pert little nose, her hair piled on top of her head, a few silky strands escaping to tease at her fragile neck. She wore a prim cream blouse and matching slacks, both of which hugged her shape enticingly.

"I like those glasses on you," he said. "Sabrina Moore, a riddle to unravel." She'd had them on during that first session he'd attended, he remembered. But not since, not until tonight.

"A riddle?" Sabrina didn't follow.

"Yeah—is the woman behind them deep? Or sultry? Thoughtful or thought-provoking? Unapproachable or...?"

She pulled her glasses off her nose and dropped them into her purse. "I didn't know I was such an enigma." Phillip had only seen the *bookish* woman, she remembered, but this man saw more. He saw the side she kept carefully concealed, the needs she didn't want to admit were there, the needs Gabe Lawrence made her so very aware of.

"Now why did you do that?" he asked. "I wanted to figure out the puzzle. Who are you, Sabrina Moore?"

"Maybe you shouldn't want to know."

Gabe was sure that was true—he shouldn't want to know. Shouldn't try to open Pandora's box. He might never get Sabrina put back inside, where she couldn't

wreak havoc with his senses, stir his hormones—
make him want what he shouldn't have.

He leaned back in his chair, a safer distance from
temptation. For a while there was only quiet between
them. He could hear the low hum of conversation
around them, the occasional hiss of the cappuccino
machine, the soft music in the background. When her
voice came, it, too, was low. And soft. And very, very
sexy.

"I'm not really a puzzle, you know. What you see
is what I am."

He leaned forward, resting both elbows on the table
and searched into her eyes. "And what is that?" He
was damned curious to know what she saw when she
looked into her soul.

"I'm a student of research. I like things clear and
concise, all fitting together in a way that makes sense.
I work hard, am maybe a little driven. I want to make
a difference in...in the only way I know how—with
my mind."

"And a very fine mind it is—but what about Sabrina the woman? What does she want?"

He pressed.

She ducked her head, obviously uncomfortable
with his question. Sabrina didn't talk much about herself—not wanting to risk...what? Emotions? Feelings? Why?

The sexy way she moistened her lower lip drove
him mad. He wasn't sure she was going to answer,
or allow him access to the inner workings of just who
Sabrina was, what she wanted from life.

She took a small sip of her coffee drink, then studied the cup. "I don't know," she answered. "I once thought I knew what I wanted."

"And that was?"

She looked up. "A family, a husband, children like the adorable ones I work with every day. But then…"

"Then what?"

She shook her head. "I was married once. It…it didn't work out." Her breath was shaky. "Phillip…met someone else."

"And now you're afraid to try again." Gabe had seen her vulnerability, her fear. He suspected she'd beaten a hasty retreat back to that institute of hers, hidden herself there within its safe walls. It was why she was afraid to relate to the children she studied—his, others—at least in any meaningful way. It just might hurt too much if she realized what she was missing out on.

He'd almost missed out, too, on Hannah and Heather's young lives, their childhood. But he'd taken the plunge, difficult though it could be at times.

Gabe was waiting for her answer, Sabrina knew. She didn't like talking about herself, dissecting her own psyche. She was more accustomed to doing that with other people's psyches, figuring out *their* lives, then trying to make sense of it in a scientific way.

It hurt to study herself—or maybe she thought she wouldn't like the conclusion she came up with. "Relationships are scary," she said. "And they aren't for everybody."

Gabe drew a breath, a long one. "I suppose I'm

living proof of *that*," he said. "But I think you're wrong about yourself, Sabrina. I've seen you with those two little girls. You have so much warmth, so much love bottled up in you. Don't sell life short because Phillip didn't know a good thing when he saw it."

She smiled. His words were like a balm to a very old wound, and she appreciated his trying to make her feel better. But she didn't know how to let her feelings out. The one time she'd tried, they'd gotten battered and bruised before they'd ever reached the surface. "Thanks for the vote of confidence, but just the same, I think I'll stick to *studying* human behavior, instead of becoming part of the confusion."

Gabe thought that a loss but he didn't say more when she folded her napkin and set it beside her half-empty coffee. "It's getting late and—"

"I know, you have a lot of work to do."

She laughed, a pretty, soft sound that he wanted to hear again, lots of times. But the cool, self-contained Sabrina was back, and Gabe had been denied access.

He returned her to her car. Tonight she'd allowed him a small glimpse of herself. The tough lady had a vulnerable side. Tough and vulnerable—a combination that was like dynamite to his resolve to stay…uninvolved.

Sabrina was sexy. Her prim-collared blouse couldn't hide the fact. Nor could his eyes deny it. The light in the parking area made her eyes look smoky, her lips full and lush. Damn, but the woman was a temptation, one Gabe knew he couldn't resist, no matter how much he knew he should.

"Sabrina..." He whispered her name a moment before he took what he had to have.

The kiss was inevitable. They had to finish what they'd started up on that mountain trail. Sabrina had wanted the kiss, needed it, if only to have one taste of Gabe. She moved toward him, into the circle of his arms, giving herself up to the emotions swirling within her, taking her where she knew she shouldn't go.

His body was hard against hers and she molded to it, fitting so right, so easily. His mouth was insistent—wanting, needing—and Sabrina responded. She parted her lips and he deepened the kiss. Heat raced through the core of her and she arched against him in the wanton pleasure of the moment. Her fingers tangled in his hair as she drew him closer, needing more of him.

He tasted like the night—dark and dangerous. It crossed her mind that this should end, but it was her body that was in control at the moment, not her mind. All the brains in the world wouldn't be defense against this man. She was out there in deep water and she didn't want to head to shore.

Gabe hadn't been prepared for the fire in her, the passion. Though he'd expected it was there, he'd misjudged its intensity. And its effect on him.

He was lost in the feel of her, wanting more, wanting *her,* this small proud woman he found such a temptation. A temptation he couldn't let get hold of him. She made him ache, she made him want. Reminding him he'd been tucked away in domesticity without the soft feel of a woman for way too long.

With a low groan of regret he drew away. "That was some kiss, lady."

She struggled for her composure. "Well, don't worry. It...it won't happen again."

Gabe wasn't so sure of that, wasn't so sure he could play it cool, not with Sabrina. Though he had two small, *very good* reasons he had to try. Hannah and Heather. He didn't need a woman muddling his mind at this juncture of his life.

Sabrina gave him a hasty good-night, then got in her car and drove away, only then remembering she hadn't set a date for her next meeting with the twins.

Another meeting—with Gabe hovering in the periphery, tempting her senses, the way he had tonight. Perhaps she should reconsider this study project—before she got hurt.

"Did you have a date with S'brina, Dad?" Hannah asked at the breakfast table the next morning.

"And can we go too next time?" her sister chimed.

Breakfast was always chaos, but this morning it was worse, Gabe decided, as the oatmeal he was fixing for the twins spattered the inside of the microwave. He'd been a bit too heavy-handed when he'd nuked it. And to add to the morning, they were out of milk. Again.

He frowned down at the twin bowls of cereal he'd dragged from the interior of the microwave. Could oatmeal be eaten without milk? he wondered. He'd always had it that way as a kid, with a warm sprinkle of cinnamon on top. Well, hell...he wasn't exactly Martha Stewart around here.

"I didn't have a date with anyone last night," he tried to explain, though he wasn't sure how the two of them had come up with the idea.

"Mrs. Chandler said she betted you had a date. That's why you wore that stuff to smell good."

He set a bowl in front of each girl. "Well, Mrs. Chandler is wrong." She was also the neighborhood busybody. And just maybe he'd have to consider getting someone else to watch the twins the next time he wanted an evening out.

"Didn't you see S'brina?"

His daughters had the tenacity of mean bulldogs and Gabe swallowed hard, remembering the heat of the kiss he'd shared with her. "Yes, but that wasn't a date, sweetheart," he told Hannah, picking up her spoon and handing it to her in the vain hope she'd dive into her cereal.

"Then why did you wear that smelly stuff?" This from Heather.

"To scare away the bears. Now, come on and eat your breakfast."

"*Da-aad!*"

The twins weren't buying that, but Gabe didn't have any good reason why he'd splashed on that new aftershave last night. Or even why he'd gone to Sabrina's talk in the first place. But he had a damned good reason for having kissed her—although by the cool, clear light of day, that reason did begin to seem a little shaky. Still, tasting those luscious lips had been a treat.

He could still see the smoky hint of want in her eyes, could still recall the soft yielding of her mouth beneath his, her curves pressing against him.

Sabrina was warm and giving. In that moment, when her guard was down, he'd seen it. He'd seen it in the way she related to the twins, as well, though she fought hard against it. What would it take to tear down that high wall she hid behind? Gabe wondered.

He didn't know. All he knew was that he was spending far too much time thinking about the lady. He had a household to run. There were the ins and outs of fatherhood to learn. *And* a half ton of work piled on his desk in the cramped corner of the den.

That.didn't leave time to fantasize about a woman. Any woman.

"Dad, is S'brina going to the park with us tomorrow?" Heather said, shoving back her cereal bowl.

She'd eaten most of it, he noted, though Hannah was still only stirring hers.

"I don't know, dear heart," he returned.

"Why don't you know?"

The two could be full of questions.

"Uh, because I forgot to ask her." And he'd meant to. In fact he'd told himself that had been his purpose for seeing her last night. To set up a session with the twins. At the park. Saturday—tomorrow.

But he wasn't so sure it was true.

Sabrina was getting to him the way no woman ever

had before. Since his divorce he'd kept what few relationships he'd had simple and uncomplicated—promising a woman nothing, expecting nothing in return.

But it could never be that way with Sabrina—she was a woman who'd want promises. And Gabe was in no position to make them.

He'd already promised two little girls he'd be there for them, no matter what. They'd lost their mother. They needed *him*. He was their anchor, their only anchor, and he'd grow barnacles before he'd let the tides sway him.

"Okay, angels, how about we give her a call this afternoon?"

He'd just have to remember to keep things strictly business between them. No more late-night kisses, no more afternoon kisses—and no more fantasies about what he'd like to do with her after the kisses.

Chapter Six

Very likely she was out of her mind. Sabrina hung up the phone, staring at it as if it were going to agree with her. Then she paced her small office, muttering colorful curses.

She'd always considered herself a sensible woman, rational. She always, *always,* weighed out a move before she took action.

So why had she kissed Gabe back last night?

Perhaps it was a little more like throwing herself at him.

And if that didn't constitute dementia, what she'd done just now certainly qualified. She'd agreed to an afternoon at the park with Hannah and Heather and their irresistible father. The one she couldn't keep her hands off of.

Or her lips.

At three this morning, after a sleepless night she

fully blamed on Gabe, she'd made the decision to forgo her study with the twins. It hadn't been an easy decision to make. The twins were sweet and adorable. Two motherless little girls who hadn't asked for any of the pain in their young lives. Tough little girls, because they'd had to be.

She'd wanted to know more about them—how they coped with their pain, how they related to their father. She'd wanted to know about Gabe, a single dad thrust into the role of being everything his daughters needed, helping them through their loss with his love and well-meaning fatherly intentions.

Who, after all, could resist the man and his irreverent daddy charm?

Certainly not her, it seemed.

All the reasons she'd wanted to do her study with the twins were the very reasons she couldn't continue. Not without losing her heart. Not without risking emotions better kept under lock and key.

It had been the sane, sensible thing to do—to bow out, now, before it was too late. And she'd patted herself on the back for making that clearheaded decision. Then the twins had called....

They'd both talked at once, sharing the receiver and trying to sound grown-up as they issued their invitation. And Sabrina had swayed like a daffodil in a stiff breeze.

Hannah and Heather touched her—in a way no other set of children ever had. And Gabe...she didn't seem to know her own mind around the man.

One more time. Just this one trip to the park because the twins had asked. Then she'd explain to Gabe, explain to the girls, that it wasn't working out.

She didn't know what reason she could give for this sudden reversal. Admit that the man tempted her senses? That he made her hot, deliciously hot, whenever she was around him—and even when she wasn't? Admit that the child psychologist was out of her element around his two darling daughters? That he'd been right, she'd seen few children from the up-close-and-personal angle?

Children's birthday parties had never been part of her social agenda, reading bedtime stories was foreign territory to her, a land mine she didn't know how to traverse. The twins' hugs, so freely given, had confused her. And the clover chain draped around her neck, a gift she'd never before received.

She hadn't had the best role models for learning warmth, for sharing feelings. She couldn't recall getting hugs as a child. Her father had been a learned man, a well-respected research biochemist, and though she'd adored him and knew he cared for her, there'd been little in the way of demonstrative affection in their home.

Her mother, a professor of art history, had never been the nurturing, cookie-baking mom. She'd demanded academic excellence from Sabrina—and it hadn't been too hard a demand to fill; study had always come easy to her.

She couldn't say the same for personal relationships, her marriage to Phillip being a prime example. Sabrina didn't know how to trust, didn't know how

to share her feelings, to share love with someone un-
conditionally.

She had tried with Phillip, perhaps not hard
enough, perhaps too late, but the result had been there
just the same. Divorce and a deeply bruised self-
image.

It was safer not to care too deeply, or share that
intimate part of herself—with anyone. It was safer to
keep emotions in check, locked carefully away, or
better yet, walled off, so there would be no chance
she'd invite new pain.

Gathering up her work, Sabrina tucked it away in
her briefcase and headed for the outer office. Violet
was watering the last plant before she, too, went home
for the weekend, home to her bustling family of five
kids and fourteen grandkids at last count.

Framed photos of them all decorated the woman's
work space and Sabrina picked up a large group picture of the family, the entire clan mugging happily
for the camera. Violet belonged intimately to all these
people. Sabrina could only wonder what that might
feel like, the warmth, the sharing. Belonging.

She set the picture back in its revered place on
Violet's desk and glanced over at her. The woman
had just finished pinching off a yellowed leaf from a
philodendron in danger of succumbing to overwater-
ing. "Are you doing anything special this weekend,
Violet?"

The woman looked up from her watering. "Special? My, yes—a big family barbecue. Tomorrow."
She paused, studying Sabrina for a moment. "Why

don't you come by, Sabrina. My Franklin's a great cook," she tempted.

Sabrina smiled at the invitation and Violet's heart of gold. "Thanks for asking but...I have plans for tomorrow."

"Oh?" Too late she caught the interested quirk of her secretary's eyebrow and knew she'd pricked Violet's curiosity. "Plans with that handsome Mr. Lawrence by any chance?"

More with his daughters, Sabrina hoped, but she didn't say so. "Just...plans," she answered. Then before Violet could question her further, she gave a quick smile and turned toward the door. "Good night, Violet. See you on Monday."

She tripped on down the hall and out into the parking lot, planning what work she wanted to do with the twins.

And wondering just what her weekend might bring.

Gabe had misgivings about the day. Not that the study Sabrina was doing might be harmful to the twins—he knew now his concern in that regard had been groundless. The twins had enjoyed her session and considered her small battery of tests nothing more than fun new games they got to play.

Tests Sabrina had designed with just that end result in mind, he suspected.

So maybe she did know a *little* something about children.

"*Hurry,* Dad. *Hurry,*" Heather said with an impatient tug on his arm, thus inhibiting his search for the keys to the 4×4.

"We're gonna be late," Hannah bossed.

"I'm sure Sabrina will wait for us—and we're not going anywhere until I find the keys," he told the girls.

They liked Sabrina, he knew. The problem was, so did he—and that had him irritable as a lion with a burr in its tail.

Still, it was no reason to take it out on the twins. He gave them a smile. "Wanna play a game, girls? Whoever finds Dad's car keys gets a...a—"

"Here they *are*, Dad." Hannah scooped them up from the small table in the hall, where he now remembered dropping them, and handed them over.

She apparently wasn't interested in her finder's fee but started toward the door. Heather gave him the fish-eye, as well, and followed after her sister.

He frowned. The two were eager to be on their way, he knew. All morning they'd been looking forward to their day at the park with Sabrina. And he supposed it was good for the girls. They needed some feminine influence in their young lives—and they'd apparently found it. This morning they'd wanted to wear ponytails "like S'brina's."

He'd caught a few other emulations, as well. Like that walk of hers, with the gentle sway of her hips, and that oh-so-feminine way she had of flipping her hair when she wore it loose.

Seeing Sabrina's grown-up ways mimicked by his two little darlings had brought a smile to his lips and a tug on his heartstrings. He wondered if Sabrina was aware of her influence on them. If she found it half as endearing as he did.

With everyone snug behind seat belts, Gabe made the trip across town, following the directions Sabrina had given him—past the institute about ten blocks, take a right, then one quick left and—

"Are we there yet?" Heather asked from the back seat.

It was the third time she'd asked in as many minutes.

"Almost."

He turned onto Sabrina's block.

"Can we get ice cream after the park?" Hannah asked.

"You had ice cream last night."

"Not with S'brina," came the reply from the back seat.

Gabe sighed.

It had the makings of a long day.

Sabrina was ready when they arrived, sitting on the front steps of her building, an intriguing redbrick, two-storied apartment house with lots of bay windows.

His mind teased at him, making him wonder which of the windows were Sabrina's. But he had no business being curious about that—today was business. And a little bit of fun for his daughters. Nothing else, he reminded himself.

Sabrina started down the walk toward them, looking as young and fresh-faced as a kid herself. She'd pulled her hair into a ponytail and tied it with a green ribbon that matched her loose-fitting shirt. Her hips curved enticingly in a pair of faded jeans, and her soft smile, a little tentative, a little shy, hit him in the gut with the force of a meteor.

Gabe opened the passenger door for her and she said a brisk hello to the twins.

"S'brina, will you push me on the big swing?" Hannah quickly asked from the back seat. "Dad doesn't push high enough."

"Me, too!" chorused her sister.

"*Dad's* just being cautious," he explained. "Too high, and you could fall out."

"He's right," Sabrina added. "But I promise to swing you high enough to get that tickle in your tummy. How's that?"

The girls believed that would be fine and Gabe thought her diplomacy was something he might want to learn. Maybe there were a few other things he could learn from her, as well. She had his two daughters entranced—and just possibly Gabe, himself.

The park was packed with children of every size. Sabrina drew a deep breath and dodged an eight-year-old intent on mowing her down on the spot.

Kids had so much energy, so much enthusiasm, enthusiasm they insisted on expressing at the tops of their very capable lungs.

Hannah and Heather were no exception. Their faces had lit up at the sight of the park, and like two kids in a candy store, who are overwhelmed by choices, the girls didn't know which piece of playground equipment they wanted to play on first. Sabrina had observed the phenomenon in the Play Lab, a much tamer version of course, but there was nothing like seeing it on this scale.

She felt herself pulled into the excitement as the twins tugged her toward a bank of swings. Gabe wore a small, amused smile. He'd found a park bench at the fringes of the chaos and settled back to rest.

Rest. She could have used his help, if not his moral support. The playground was a land mine of activity—and she'd come into it unarmed.

She tugged her gaze away from Gabe and concentrated on the twins and the task of swinging them toward the clouds. Their small legs pumped air and their whoops of delight sent a warm flutter through her. She'd brought a couple of personality tests for them to take, an attempt to learn more about how the two siblings bonded with each other, but she was sure she'd find some quiet moment to administer the tests later.

When they'd moved on to the giant slide, her glance again returned to Gabe. He looked far too comfortable on that park bench, both arms extended across the back of it, long denim-clad legs stretched out in front. A playful breeze tugged at his hair, catching the strands and ruffling the ends like a feather. Two days ago she'd caught her hands in its thickness as she'd kissed him back.

What had possessed her to act so foolishly? To lose

herself in the feel of him, the taste of him? To wrap herself in his arms—?

"Catch me, catch me, S'brina," Heather called from the top of the big slide and Sabrina jerked her attention away, placing it where it belonged—on the twins.

Where she needed to keep it.

Hannah followed down the slide in quick succession and Sabrina gave herself up to the moment. She was having fun—in spite of everything.

The sun beat down warmly on her face and arms and she caught the whiff of pine in the air, the wind blowing it fresh and clean through the park's stand of trees. She couldn't ask for a better afternoon to be out-of-doors, to feel alive.

"Here comes Dad," Heather said, pointing in Gabe's general direction.

"You're not s'posed to point," Hannah corrected her sister.

"It's okay if you're *outdoors.*"

"Is not—you made that up."

"Did not." Heather held her ground.

Their argument gave Sabrina pause. "What about twin bonding?" she asked Gabe who'd heard the tail end of the twins' sibling feud.

"You're the psychologist," he said with a hint of a smile tempting his lips. "You tell me."

She'd like to tell him a thing or two, and the first would be that he was standing too close. She could see the silver flecks dance in his blue eyes, the small razor nick on the right side of his chin, the slight twitch to his lips as he tried to keep from laughing outright at her fluster.

It seemed she thought she knew all there was to know about twins and Gabe was effectively showing her the other side of the coin. "You're enjoying this, aren't you? Showing up the doctor with your daddy expertise."

His grin broadened. "Immensely. Don't worry, though," he said, leaning in closer as if he were about to divulge a secret. "Your theory isn't totally blown out of the water. Despite their sisterly fighting, those two are really thicker than thieves. Just try and separate them and you'll find out. The bond exists."

She wondered how the man had gotten so smart.

And what all she could learn from him, if only she dared.

When the afternoon drew to an end, Sabrina realized she'd gotten very little in the way of *formal* research done. She'd observed much about the twins, from their sibling spats to their fierce independence. She'd even glimpsed a little of that sibling bond that Gabe had spoken of.

But the body of her work, the hard data, that would turn a study from mere observation into a well-rounded treatise on twin behavior, had been lost. She'd abandoned it in favor of enjoyment, having fun with Gabe's girls.

Now she would have to set up another time with them, something she'd promised herself she wouldn't do.

Gabe had been a major distraction, as well. He either left her alone with the kids to fall on her face or he was there beside her, hovering too close for her senses, oozing charm and creating a definite diversion.

She wasn't sure who had sabotaged her work—the twins or Gabe—but it had happened.

And now she had a price to pay.

She turned to Gabe as they left the park. "I hope you know I haven't gotten a lick of real work done today."

The look on her face made Gabe feel a small twinge of guilt about that. "You got distracted by swings and slides and two little sisters, huh?"

She nodded and gave the park one small, last wistful glance—as if she might have left a part of herself back there.

Gabe observed her closely, wondering what it was that stirred in her mind, in her thoughts. But he doubted Sabrina would tell him or that she'd even reveal it to herself.

He knew his two little cherubs were getting to her, tugging at the heart she didn't want touched. Why? What was Sabrina frightened of?

What made her keep that forever safe distance from everything except her work?

"Look," he said. "I'll give you time this evening to finish up with the twins." A few strands of her hair had come loose from her ponytail and coiled around her face in tiny curls, her lips pink with the day's excitement. "We'll stop and pick up a pizza for dinner. After we eat and the girls have their bath, I'll turn them—and my den—over to you.''

Sabrina gave his offer a moment of thought. She *had* wanted to finish up. It was her afternoon plan that had gone dangerously awry. However, this prospect didn't seem a whole lot safer.

The scene Gabe painted fell under the heading of *cozy, intimate*—and Sabrina wasn't so sure she could handle either.

"Did you have other plans?" he asked.

"No. No plans."

"Then it's a deal?"

Sabrina hesitated, torn between wanting to salvage what she could of the study before she abandoned it, and her need to exercise good sense. Giving up her time with the twins would be hard enough without being roped in further now, without more memories to stir in her mind when she was no longer part of this little family's life.

Gabe was waiting for her answer. And so were Hannah and Heather, whose ears had pricked at the word *pizza*.

"I want pepp'roni," Hannah announced from the back seat. "Can we get pepp'roni, pleeeze?"

Sabrina doubted either girl would grasp the concept of *no*. Not when their father had mentioned pizza.

"I don't like pepp'roni," Heather voiced.

"It's okay—you can pick off the pieces," her sister told her, which made Heather's little face pucker.

Gabe saved the day—or at least a few tears. "How about we get two kinds? Sabrina?"

He was demanding an answer from her, a wry
smile teasing at his lips, as if he knew she wouldn't
be able to refuse. Not his two little darlings.

His babies were playing havoc with her life—and
Sabrina wasn't sure it would ever be the same again.

"Two pizzas—sure, why not?" she gave in.

As if she'd had a choice.

Gabe smiled and reached for the car phone to call
in their order.

A short while later the little group trooped into
Gabe's kitchen, taste buds watering. Gabe hurried
around, getting everyone napkins, forks and something to drink—milk for the twins, a little red wine
for Sabrina and himself.

Sabrina tried to gather her wits about her and not
give in to the homey feel of the setting...Gabe's
young daughters, both eager to talk at once, and
Gabe—who'd settled across the table from her.

His hair was mussed, as if by a lover's hand, and
his skin glowed from the out-of-doors. The man was
a force to be reckoned with—even over pizza with
his daughters. She reminded herself not to be caught
alone with him. He'd bowl her over and leave her
flattened.

"Tell me about these tests you designed—and why
the twins seem to think they're games," Gabe queried.

She laughed. "Because they *are* games." Sabrina
felt herself relax. She didn't know if it was the wine
or because Gabe had asked her about her work, which
was something she could talk about comfortably. "I

knew I could hold young children's attention spans longer, and learn more about them, if they were doing what children do best—play.''

''I'd say that was clever thinking.'' Gabe wondered if the same concept could apply to getting them to clean up their room, the Saturday-morning chore that usually ended in a standoff, with him looking like the ogre of the day for even suggesting it.

''It seems to work,'' Sabrina added. ''And I'm usually pleased with the results.''

''So how does drawing boxes in little circles, and such, tell you anything about twin behavior?''

She smiled. ''That's a little more complicated.''

''So, try me.''

Sabrina was surprised to find him interested in what she did. She'd received more than a few awards for her innovative child-testing procedure, but she didn't tell Gabe that. ''It tells me such things as intelligence, how one sibling relates to another, which child is dominant, which child thinks for him or herself and which one is content to follow.''

''All from little boxes?''

''I told you it was complicated.''

''So how do my twins stack up?''

Sabrina glanced over the heads of the little blond-haired beauties as the two ate their favorite pizzas. They giggled with each other, apparently not intrigued by the adult conversation around them. Still, she knew little pitchers had big ears. ''I'll get back to you on that one,'' she answered.

Gabe caught her meaning. ''Later,'' he said, and

Sabrina wondered how that single word could sound so sensual coming from his lips and conjure up alternative meanings in her mind.

She told parents all the time how their little darlings fared in her Play Lab, but a one-on-one with Gabe held other import.

"The pizza is great," she said, and took another bite, not wanting to think too deeply about any quiet meeting with this parent.

"Can I have another slice?" asked Heather. She had pizza sauce all around her mouth and Sabrina reached to dab it away with her napkin.

It was a gesture not missed by Gabe. Sabrina looked so natural here with his children. She looked as if she belonged in their kitchen, sharing pizza.

Maybe it hadn't been such a great idea inviting her back here tonight, he thought.

"How about a small slice?" he suggested to Heather. "So you're not up all night with a tummy ache."

Heather agreed to that and Gabe cut a small piece off for her.

"How about you, Hannah?" he asked his other daughter with a smile.

"I'm full," she said. "Now can we play S'brina's games?"

"As soon as you finish your milk and have your bath," he told them both.

Chapter Seven

Bath time was not an easy ritual in the Lawrence household. Gabe was always reminded of the fact that mommies were probably better prepared for this sort of thing, with their gentle hands and their soft voices. With daddies there were usually tears from soap in the eyes, towels that were "too scratchy" and water all over the bathroom floor.

While he made sure the two got some semblance of clean, Sabrina set up her games in the den. They'd taken longer than usual over pizza, the kids *and* himself tempted to linger tonight because of their dinner guest. But Gabe didn't want the twins to get sleepy before she got her promised time with them.

"We want S'brina to brush our hair," Hannah said. "You pull the tangles, Dad."

Gabe grinned as he got the last twin into comfy

pj's. He supposed he could share that job duty with Sabrina—if she didn't mind the task.

He hadn't expected this evening to seem so...intimate, but it was stacking up that way. He hadn't expected a woman to look so right in his house, not after months of just the three of them.

And not just any woman—but Sabrina.

Quickly Gabe curtailed the thought.

They were doing fine as they were. He was doing his daddy thing—and finding it more rewarding than he'd ever expected.

The twins missed Meg, he knew. Gabe didn't do everything right—like detangling their wind-tousled hair after a trip to the park—but they were accepting him as a parent. As their dad.

He wished with all his heart they could have grown up with both a mother and a father, a happy little family circle like he and his sister had enjoyed, but life didn't always work out the way one expected. Sometimes circumstances called the shots.

"Okay, brush your teeth," he told the girls. "And I'll go check with Sabrina about the hairbrushing thing."

He left them fighting over the sink and went to see what Sabrina was doing.

He found her sitting in the center of the floor in his den, arranging her "games" around her. She'd moved some of his things out of the way—the old footstool he liked because it was all broken in, his set of golf clubs he never found time to put to use anymore, a stack of magazines, unread of late.

She hadn't touched his art board set up in front of
the window, something else he hadn't had time to
utilize as much as he'd like. Work had definitely
taken a back seat to the twins. But school would be
starting soon, then the house would be quiet again.
Probably too quiet, he suspected. Without hearing the
twins' laughter, their squabbles, time would creep by.
He could take on some new projects then, search for
some new accounts.

Sabrina looked up, noticing his glance around the
room. She flushed slightly. "I hope you don't mind
that I...I moved a few things," she said. "I'll put
everything back, of course. When I'm finished here."

The soft glow from the lamp brought out gold
strands in her hair and glistened across her intelligent
face. Her lips looked full and ripe enough to kiss and
desire surged in his groin, hot and low and insistent.
He wanted her, wanted her even though it was the
wrong time and she was the wrong woman. With Sabrina, work came first. Even above two little girls.

He hoped that thought would cool his socks.

"Don't worry," he said. "I think you improved the
place."

She grinned, the smile stealing onto her lips as if
unbidden.

"Are...are the girls ready?"

"Yes—*no*. They...have a request."

"A request?"

He folded his arms and leaned against the doorjamb, wishing she didn't look so inviting, so in control of his den, so right there. "It, uh, seems they

think Dad is wicked with a hairbrush. Their curly locks need a woman's touch. Do you mind doing the honors?"

"They want me?"

"They want you."

She glanced down at her work set out around her, as if she thought it might disappear, then she nodded. "Sure. I think I can handle that."

"Don't do too good a job," he cautioned. "They'll be stuck with me again when you're not here, and I'll get nothing but complaints about my handiwork."

There was a teasing grin on his face. Sabrina knew he meant to be humorous, but his remark served to remind her that after tonight—if she was able to complete what she hoped to do—she wouldn't be around.

He was right. The girls shouldn't get attached to her. She was only a friend, one passing through their young lives only briefly. She wasn't sure why that made her feel so sad, but it did.

Little by little Gabe's daughters had chipped away at her reserve, until it was now a shaky barrier, one that could allow her feelings to leak out. And pain to surge in.

How had she let that happen?

And Gabe. She would miss him, too. His humor. The way his eyes brightened at the sight of the twins. She'd miss witnessing his efforts at fatherhood and his determination to be the best parent he could be, his daughters' knight in shining armor whenever they needed him—and even when they didn't. The image brought a smile to her lips. And a pang of admiration for the man he was.

"I don't think I'm probably very good at this myself," she said softly.

"Ah, I bet you are."

He strode across the room and helped her up from her sitting position on the floor. The touch of his hand was warm as he offered it to her. His arm encircled her waist as she stood, just a brush of support at the small of her back, but it was not without its effect on her. His eyes looked so very blue up close, a sapphire lake a woman could drown in if she wasn't careful.

Sabrina stepped away from his touch, gingerly making her way across her carefully laid-out papers and games. "I won't be long," she said.

She found the twins dressed in pink seersucker jammies. Even their bedwear came matched, she thought. But this time, instead of annoyance, she let a small smile touch her lips.

"I understand there are two little girls who need a—" She stopped herself. The word *mommy* almost came to her lips. "—a little help with a hairbrush," she finished safely.

The near slip bothered her. Not only did it surprise her that she could feel motherly toward the girls— toward *any* child—but it also filled her mind that no woman could replace the mother they had lost. Her hapless comment would have hurt.

Hannah bustled over to greet her, hairbrush waving in the air. "Do me, do me first," she begged.

That brought a loud complaint from Heather. "She gets to be first all the time."

"I don't think she's first *all* the time, Heather, but I do think it's your turn to be first this time. Is that okay with you, Hannah?" she asked, turning to the other twin with an ameliorating smile.

Hannah allowed that it was. She said so cheerfully, which showed she had a gracious side. It also told Sabrina that these two could put aside their sibling rivalry on occasion—and give their father a break, at least once in a while.

Heather scooted onto the chair in front of the dressing table in their small bedroom and met Sabrina's gaze in the mirror. "I like you," she said, totally off the cuff.

It caught Sabrina by surprise, and she felt something well up in her chest. She blinked to hold back a quick sting of tears at the touching compliment. "And I like *you*," she answered. "In fact, no one's ever said a nicer thing to me."

"In your whole life?"

"In my whole life."

"I like you, too," voiced Hannah, not to be outdone by her sister. She jumped off the end of the bed to swing her arms around Sabrina's waist.

The rivalry could have been humorous but Sabrina didn't feel like laughing. How was she ever going to find the strength to walk away from these two special little girls? Kneeling down to child level she hugged them both.

"Now I think we'd better get you looking all pretty," she said.

The brushing ritual went remarkably well and the time was filled with chatter from the two, sometimes sweet, sometimes boisterous, and Sabrina adored every moment of it.

"Our mommy brushed our hair every night," Hannah said quietly as Sabrina pulled the brush through her child-soft curls, too. "Sometimes at night Heather cries for her."

Sabrina ached inside for Hannah, realizing the little girl didn't want to admit to being less than brave, didn't want to admit to her own vulnerabilities. "Only Heather?" she asked gently, sure she knew the answer.

"Well, sometimes me, too." Her little voice came soft and low and Sabrina pictured her hugging her twin, trying to be the big, "older" sister, while inside she hurt, too.

Sabrina laid down the hairbrush and pulled both twins to her. "Oh, sweeties, it's all right to miss your mommy. It's all right to cry for her. She was very important in your life and you loved her. We all miss those we loved.

"But your mommy wouldn't want you to be too sad. She'd want you to be happy, happy with your dad since she can't be here."

"Did...did you know our mom?" Heather asked.

Sabrina gave her a slow smile. "No, honey, I didn't know your mom. But I do know she loved you both very, very much."

Heather gave a soft smile then and put her small arms around Sabrina's neck. Hannah hugged her, too. And Sabrina held them both, wishing she knew how to take all their pain away.

"The twins are a little tired," Sabrina said when she joined Gabe in the kitchen a short while later. "I left them in the bedroom with a promise that you would come tuck them in. I can do the games with them some other evening."

She knew she'd somehow committed herself to these two children, that the time wasn't right to walk away. And she doubted she could have, even if she'd had to.

She started for the den to gather up her things but Gabe stopped her. He took her arms, holding her to the spot.

"I heard, Sabrina. I heard what you said to the twins...and I think you are wonderful." There was emotion in his low, deep voice and a softness in his eyes as he gazed down at her. "Very possibly you accomplished more with my daughters here tonight than I have in the past six months they've been with me."

"Oh, Gabe, I didn't mean to overstep any bounds."

He smiled and ran his hands up and down her arms. "You didn't overstep anything." He paused a long moment. "Thanks, Sabrina."

His words, his smile, his thank-you, meant more to her than the world. Seeing the admiration in his eyes moved her to cloud nine, floating there on his praise.

"I—I'm just glad I could help. I wanted to help the twins in some way, not just take from them for my study. I promised you that."

"Oh, I think this went beyond any study, any promise. This came from the heart of who you are. Who you really are, Sabrina."

Her emotions, her feelings for the twins, had been there in her tonight, Gabe thought. Laid bare for his daughters to see, for him to see. This had nothing to do with the psychologist she was, the research she did. This was human and warm and full of feeling, and Gabe wouldn't let her hide it behind the banner of work, of just doing her job.

He hadn't intended to kiss her—until that moment. But he doubted an avalanche could have stopped him. He'd gotten a rare glimpse of the real Sabrina tonight and he very much liked what he saw.

She was warm and sweet and feminine, and as he drew her closer, fitting her soft curves to the length of him, he realized just how feminine. His lips tasted her mouth, his tongue teased and tangled with hers, and his body reacted in the most elemental way.

Cupping her denimed bottom with the palms of his hands he pulled her hard against him—and it was nearly his undoing. He let out a low groan of need and deepened the kiss.

Sabrina relished the feel of this man, his closeness, the heat of him. His touch, his kisses, felt so right, so very right, though there was no earthly reason why they should. She swallowed his low groan of need that tore from his throat, a need that was further evidenced by the hard feel of him against her. She'd stirred that very male response in him and it excited her.

She wanted to go with the feelings screaming through her body, the desire pounding hot in her blood, but she knew two little girls who were not asleep as yet. It wouldn't do to have them stroll in and find her locked in a heated embrace with their dad.

"Gabe, we…the twins—"

"I know. *Could walk in.* Those two will keep us honest, I'm afraid." He drew a slow, ragged breath. "Let me take you home, Sabrina…and we can finish what we started here. I'll call Mrs. Benjamin to sit with the girls—"

"Gabe, no. I don't think…. I mean, I think I should take a cab home. That would be best." She couldn't take him away from the twins, out into the night to drive her home, not when the girls were sleepy and would be wanting their dad. Neither could she let herself be alone with him, totally alone. Gabe was right; their little chaperones would keep them—at least *her*—honest.

Gabe could feel Sabrina pull away, retreat behind that impenetrable wall of hers where she hid all her feelings, all those beautiful emotions she'd let slip tonight. She'd given to the twins. And just now, to him, and he wanted more of her.

"Don't run," he said, his voice more entreaty than command. He touched a tangled curl that teased at her face, thinking how frightened she looked at that moment. "You're so beautiful," he whispered softly. "Inside and out. I saw that tonight. Don't run from that. Don't hide it away."

"Sometimes...sometimes it's better to hide emotions, at least ones we don't understand."

"What don't you understand, Sabrina? What happens when I kiss you, when I hold you? God, when I just *touch* you," he added.

Her answer was a soft nod of her head and a breathy yes, and he wanted to take her in his arms again. He wanted to kiss her until it all became clear what he was fighting, had been fighting—and was losing. He stroked her cheek, his hand trembling as it made a path over the heated blush of her skin.

"I don't understand what's happening between us, either, Sabrina. But I do know I can't run from it."

She came softly into his arms and he held her, just held her, hoping the heat of his body would stop the tremors in hers. Her pliant curves pressed against him had him rock hard and wanting her more than ever. He fought down the urge, hot desire that threatened to take precedence over any good sense he might have left.

She melted against him for what seemed an eternity, yet at the same time, far too brief. Then she drew away, leaving him aching, empty, in raw need, and went to gather up her things.

He let her go and went to the phone to call Mrs. Benjamin and explain that he couldn't let his dinner guest get home on her own, that the twins were sleepy and already in their pj's. The woman would be curious, he knew, but he didn't want Sabrina going home alone.

He'd leave her at her door, without another kiss, until he could figure out these confusing emotions of his, and Sabrina was less frightened of hers.

It would be the hardest thing he ever did.

Sabrina knew it was fruitless to protest further about taking a cab. Gabe had been too quick for her, installing the grandmotherly Mrs. Benjamin in residence before she could belabor the point.

Didn't she usually lose with this man?

She'd slipped into the twins' bedroom to tell them good-night, then Gabe trailed in after, tucking his children in and explaining if they needed anything, Mrs. B. was there. Around a sleepy yawn the girls wanted to know why they couldn't go along to "take S'brina home."

"You'd be asleep before you'd gone a block," he told his little blond beauties, then gave them each a noisy smooch, which made them giggle, and flickered on their angel night-light.

He escorted Sabrina out of the room and past Mrs. B. who seemed all too curious about her. Sabrina gave the older woman a quick goodbye before Gabe ushered her out into the night. "She's great with the twins," he said. "But definitely the neighborhood Mrs. Pry-inski. I'll have to give her a full account when I return, I'm sure. In fact, she'll probably be clocking the trip to your house, to see how long I linger on your doorstep."

Sabrina figured she'd have a few questions of her own to answer on Monday morning—to Violet. And a few to answer to herself—tonight. When she was alone. When Gabe had gone, back to his house and his girls.

Everything in her life had seemed so much simpler before—before she'd fallen for Gabe and his two little daughters.

She'd only been kidding herself about being able to walk away at the end of the study project, a dangerous miscalculation on her part.

She had wanted Gabe's kiss tonight. Too much. She liked having him hold her, exulted in the hard feel of him. And she wasn't at all sure she could resist him on her doorstep. Wasn't sure she was strong enough to send him home—before the wily Mrs. B. had the evening clocked as a tryst and Gabe as a man of…action.

Silence reigned as Gabe drove, except for a mellow tune on the car radio. Something mind jangling and raucous would have matched Sabrina's thoughts better at the moment. She leaned her head back, hoping the music would soothe her, gentle her mood and her mind. But her mind raced on tumultuously, over the evening, Gabe's kiss, these feelings that confused and frightened her.

She tried to censor her awareness of the man beside her, the play of his strong, broad hands on the steering wheel, his sexy wrists, the light of the night slanting across his face, his sensual mouth skewed slightly, as if he, too, were deep in confusing thought.

She wanted to speak, to break the tension between them, put things back on an easier footing, but no words came.

Finally they reached her apartment and Gabe pulled to a stop at the curb.

"About us..." he said as he walked her to the door.

She stopped and turned around to look at him, certain what was to come had to do with tonight, and the emotions it had unleashed. The glow from the porch light splayed over his rugged features. His blue eyes looked dark, nearly navy, and his mouth enticing. She knew its feel—and its effect on her senses.

"Gabe, whatever happened between us..."

He'd followed her up the last porch step and stood beside her.

This close he was devastating. Her heart thudded against her rib cage and she fought down the urge to moisten her suddenly dry lips. Why could this man leave her so breathless? What hold did he have on her?

And why couldn't she break it?

He reached as if to touch her cheek, then thought better of it and rammed his hands deep in his pockets. "Something happens whenever we're together," he said. "Something I'll be damned if I understand— and I'd have to be a fool not to know you feel it, too."

"Yes." Her single word came softly, almost inaudibly.

What was Gabe saying? And what could she answer?

What emotions, feelings, would she have to admit to? And did she dare? If she spoke them, she could never get them back, her mind screamed.

She'd meant what she'd said earlier. It was better not to confront emotions you didn't understand. It was her way, and she liked to think that it had protected her through the years, protected her from hurt, from too much pain—even with Phillip. "Maybe it would be better if we didn't discuss it right now," she said. "I mean, it's probably just that we've been thrown together because—because of the twins."

He gave her a long considering look. "Yeah," he said finally. "Yeah, that's probably it."

Sabrina thought he looked relieved, and she was surprised at the quick stab of pain that caused her. Did she want there to be more between them?

Of course not.

"I should give you time alone with the twins," he went on. "At least…until these feelings die a natural death."

"Yes," she answered. It was an attempt to sound pragmatic, though it was far from what she was feeling on the inside.

"In fact, it was what you wanted from the start," he added.

She'd wanted more than that. She'd wanted to do the study in her nice, safe Play Lab. Away from a handsome father who could turn her inside out with one simple kiss, who could confuse her and make her want to run for cover, yet still stick around and steal one more kiss, one more moment in his arms.

One more…whatever else he was offering.

Gabe touched her cheek and Sabrina felt every ridge in his fingertips. When he moved to her lower lip, brushing its fullness, heat raced to her feminine core. He ignited every nerve ending, every dormant want and need in her body with that one soft, gentle gesture.

"Thanks for tonight," he said, his voice low and whiskey rough. "Thanks for what you said to Hannah and Heather."

As he walked away, back to his car, she knew she wanted more from this man than his appreciation. With a slow sigh, she turned and went inside.

Chapter Eight

It had been an awful week so far. Gabe had paced the floor four nights running and he was no closer to solving the dilemma he faced. Things had heated up between Sabrina and him. There was no doubt about that. And he'd promised himself he wouldn't involve a woman, any woman, in his life until he and the twins were on surer footing, until Hannah and Heather felt secure in their new home and he'd become the dad he'd never been for them.

But Sabrina had slipped past that resolve, and he wasn't sure how it had happened. He only knew that it had—big-time—and that it was costing him in sleepless nights.

He'd tried not to let his unwanted insomnia impact on the twins, but his advertising accounts were definitely suffering. The house wasn't too clean these days, either, and the wash had piled up knee-high to a water tower in the laundry room. He cooked for the twins, but somehow forgot to eat something himself.

There seemed no answer to his middle-of-the-night deliberations with his conscience. The way he saw it, he was faced with two choices, both of them laced with problems and more ill effects than he wanted to consider.

He could allow Sabrina one last session, maybe two, with the twins—time to hopefully finish up her project. Then, all of them go their separate ways. She, to do her research. He, to continue playing Mr. Mom—*and*, somewhere in all that daddy detail, find the time to run an ad agency.

But he and Sabrina were not the only two involved here. The twins had accepted her—more than accepted, they adored her. And Gabe would be the bad guy if he were to end the relationship.

Not only would he be the villain, but the twins would feel the loss of Sabrina's kindness, her gentleness, her feminine influence—not to mention that on-target wisdom she could dish out when the twins confided their pain to her. They'd lost Meg all too recently. To lose Sabrina because Gabe thought it best, would be another setback in their adjustment to life and the real world.

His second choice—to continue seeing Sabrina—would be a problem of another sort. There was no doubt, if the relationship continued, he would make love to her. And life would get complicated for all of them.

He'd be splitting his days—and nights—between

the twins and spending time with Sabrina. Alone. The two of them, getting to know each other as a man and woman should.

He'd be reneging on his promise to Hannah and Heather that he would be there for them, no matter what. One hundred percent. Just the three of them—through thick and thin.

And if the relationship with Sabrina failed? What then? What would happen to the twins if this involvement went the way of many, down the drink—the way his marriage to Meg had?

Gabe had just emerged from the laundry room—in the middle of washing everything they owned—to find Hannah on the phone.

He hadn't even heard it ring.

Hannah was telling whoever had called that her dad couldn't come to the phone, he was doing the laundry "because she and her sister were out of clean jammies and—"

Gabe snatched the phone away before she could add the remainder of the conversation he'd had with her a few minutes earlier.

"I was just telling Mr. Win...Windbag we didn't have clean *panties*," she said with a bewildering wail.

Gabe groaned. "It's Winfield, not...Wind*bag*," he told her, then asked her to go play nicely with Heather—and took the call from the man threatening to pull his account from Gabe's agency.

He wondered just where this conversation would have gone from there, had he not intervened when he had. Hannah liked to tell everything she knew—un-censored—whenever she got the chance.

"Hello, Mr. Winfield," he said into the receiver, hoping Hannah hadn't killed the account for him.

He quickly apologized for his daughter. Winfield wasn't the kind of man who'd find conversation with a six-year-old endearing. He was a confirmed bachelor—and a grumpy one at that.

Ten minutes later Gabe hung up from the call and sank into the nearest chair, massaging his temples in a vain effort to relieve the headache that had begun to pound there.

Winfield had been vocal about what he wanted from Gabe, and that was no less than his full attention on the ad campaign Winfield had been promised—which included Gabe hopping the first flight to Kansas City and seeing to the account *in person*.

Gabe cursed inventively and considered telling the man he couldn't work with him.

The twins needed him. In the past six months he'd never had to leave them overnight, not once—and he didn't like it that business was pulling him away now.

But he needed to do a good job for Winfield. The man could hurt him professionally. A bad mark in this competitive business could be the death knell.

Forty-five minutes later he had his portfolio case filled with design ideas he hoped would soothe the ruffled feathers of the man in Kansas City. And he'd tossed a couple changes of clothes in an overnighter, along with a razor and toothbrush. But…he had no sitter.

Well, that wasn't quite true. Mrs. B. was available until tomorrow. She'd even agreed to finish up the laundry. But bright and early in the morning, her son and daughter-in-law were picking her up for a week at their cabin in Estes Park.

Gabe knew there was no way he could finish with Winfield and be back by then.

He'd tried his list of trusted moms around the neighborhood, but none was available. And he couldn't leave his daughters with just anyone.

Maybe he should have employed a live-in housekeeper, he thought, instead of stubbornly insisting he could do this fatherhood thing solo.

With a low groan Gabe wondered how Mr. Winfield felt about having a cute little pair of twins tag along on a business trip.

Sabrina spent part of the afternoon studying the Nelson trio. The unruly little boys were a big contrast to Hannah and Heather. She smiled just thinking about them—Gabe's little girls, so sweet and vulnerable, so tough and brave. They'd taken Sabrina into their confidence and it was an honor Sabrina didn't take lightly.

They missed their mother. Hannah had confided that, as difficult as it had been for her to admit to being less than the tough "older" sister.

Sabrina had felt for them both, felt their ripping pain tear through her heart. She'd wanted to help, had wanted to make everything right for them somehow, but in reality her words had seemed so inadequate.

Gabe had pronounced her wonderful. His praise warmed her still, though she wasn't sure she deserved it.

Gabe. He hadn't been far from her thoughts. That much was evident by her scattered mind, her tardiness for staff meetings with her peers and superiors. And her inability to control the Nelson trio—as now, with Nathan throwing blocks across the floor and Barry and Devon laughing with sheer delight at their brother's antics.

When had she lost control of this afternoon? she wondered. Maybe it was time to return them to their mother—past time.

"That's enough for today, children," she said, gathering up her notes. "We'll play again next week."

She buzzed for Violet, handed her the notes she'd taken, then herded the three out the door and back to their mom who waited for them across the hall.

Sabrina could feel a growing sympathy for the young mother, realizing only too well why she looked harried. The hour Sabrina spent with the three was probably the only rest the woman got.

"I hope they behaved for you, Dr. Moore," Mrs. Nelson said as the boys charged toward her.

Sabrina watched in apprehension as they threatened to tackle their mom around the knees. "Well, let's just say they were a little…high-strung."

Their mother sighed. "I should have one-tenth their energy."

Sabrina bid them goodbye, feeling a moment of guilt that she could escape and Mrs. Nelson could not.

Or was it relief?

Violet caught up to her in the hallway, having just finished restoring the Play Lab. "Those three need straitjackets," she grumbled.

"Isn't that a little extreme?" Sabrina gave her an arched look.

Violet regarded the trio, playing hide-and-seek around their mother's skirted legs, nearly toppling her over, as she headed toward the door. "No, just...*effective*."

Sabrina grinned at her secretary, who was usually warm and kindly. Apparently the Nelson children brought out the worst in her. "I take it you didn't raise any boys with that much *enthusiasm?*"

"Enthusiasm? Is that what you doctors call it these days?" Violet frowned and ducked into her office to type up her notes.

Sabrina headed for the coffee room, needing one good strong cup before she finished up her work for the day.

She'd postponed phoning Gabe and setting up another session with the twins until now, when hopefully she would have a moment to catch a rational breath.

She no longer tried to hide the fact that she enjoyed her time with Hannah and Heather, couldn't deny it to herself if she had to. Neither could she deny her attraction to Gabe.

What she was going to do about *him* was a matter she hadn't yet considered.

By the time she carried her coffee into her office, Violet was already hard at work typing the notes for the day. Sabrina wasn't sure what she'd do without the woman's efficiency, her ability to decipher even the most disjointed note taking and her friendship.

Sabrina had always been too busy to establish any real network of friends. She usually limited her liaisons to the small, close-knit group she worked with at the institute. They seemed to understand her drive, her need to work, her interests.

But lately she'd found herself wanting more than just work in her life. She wasn't sure when she'd first noticed the restlessness—but she had the feeling that Gabe Lawrence and his little darlings had opened up the door, had made her see a certain…joy in the world.

With a slow smile she set her coffee cup on the desk and picked up the phone, needing very much to hear Gabe's voice.

He answered on the first ring.

"Is something wrong?" she asked him, hearing his quick, clipped tone. For one tense moment she feared something had happened to the twins, that they'd had an accident, or were sick, but Gabe quickly assured her that both girls were fine.

"I—I wanted to schedule a session to work with the twins, but perhaps I should wait until a better time," she said.

Gabe didn't sound at all like himself.

"Is—is there something I can do?" she added. The man sounded as harried as Mrs. Nelson had looked, leaving the institute with her riotous threesome.

"Do? Know any good baby-sitters?" he asked.

It wasn't a stock item Sabrina usually kept in her Rolodex. "I take it Mrs. Benjamin isn't available?"

"Nor anyone else it seems," he answered, frustration evident in his voice.

"Gabe, look...I haven't had a lot of practice at baby-sitting, but if you need to go out tonight, I could come by. I want to finish up my project with the twins anyway and—"

"It's not a matter of just a few hours, Sabrina. More like a few days." He explained about his necessary trip to Kansas City and that he'd never left the twins overnight before—with anyone.

Mothers with demanding jobs faced similar problems, and it tore their heart out to leave their child. Sabrina heard the same note of anguish in Gabe's voice.

"Gabe, let me stay with them. I'd enjoy it. The girls would enjoy it and you'd be free to do your job."

He let out a slow sigh, but didn't answer her. Did he think she couldn't handle the situation? Did he think her incapable? The unspoken possibility stung.

"Sabrina, you're exactly what I need, but I—I can't ask you—"

"And why not?" She wished he'd meant something more with his words, "you're exactly what I need." For one quick moment she realized she wanted to feel his little family belonged to her and she to them, that they *needed* her.

It took a little more persuasion, but Sabrina got Gabe to relent and let her play baby-sitter for the girls. Her Thursday schedule looked light, so light she could easily rearrange it, and Fridays were reserved for her personal activities anyway. As for her weekend, should Gabe's business meeting drag on, it was free, too. She'd purposely kept it that way, hoping she could see the twins. Now she'd have plenty of time with them—while Gabe was away.

It was only after she hung up from talking with Gabe, after she'd committed herself to the task, that fear began to creep in.

What did she know about taking care of children? Really know?

"The young lady who was here for dinner last week?"

Mrs. Benjamin's curiosity topped the Richter scale and Gabe drew a breath. "Yes, one and the same."

The woman had insisted on coming over to help with the laundry and keep one eye on the twins until Sabrina arrived, leaving Gabe with nothing to do but answer Mrs. B.'s questions and wonder if he'd done the right thing in having Sabrina stay with the girls.

The girls, of course, thought it wonderful, and even acquiesced to clean their room in honor of her visit.

As soon as he returned from Kansas City, he would look into hiring a live-in housekeeper. He could not continue to impose on Sabrina or Mrs. B., or even the other moms in the neighborhood, although he did return the favor with the latter by watching their kids when the need arose.

He just wasn't all that sure he liked the idea of adding a fourth person to their family threesome. It would change things. He liked having the girls depend on *him*, a consideration he'd never entertained when they were babies and Meg was there.

What had he missed in those early years?

By the time Gabe had an airline ticket reserved and waiting for him at the airport and had paced the carpet in his den more than two dozen times, he heard the doorbell peal, heralding Sabrina's arrival.

He hurried to the front door and swung it open, realizing he was eager to see her.

She stood on the threshold, a small tan suitcase in hand, and a smile on her face that didn't quite reach her eyes. Was she regretting her offer to stay with the girls? Was that trepidation he read in her gaze?

He could certainly understand if it was. He'd known fear at the prospect of caring for two little girls himself. But he thought women had a built-in facility for nurturing and stuff.

Perhaps it wasn't the case.

"Having second thoughts? It's not too late to back out," he told her.

He could toss some clothes into a bag and take the twins with him—though it would no doubt offend Mr. Winfield's sensibilities.

He'd just have to explain to the man that it couldn't be helped.

"Second thoughts? Of course not," she denied, and Gabe studied her expression for proof of that.

He wasn't sure he quite believed her, but Sabrina was sticking to her story.

"Come in," he said.

He took her bag and drew her inside.

She smelled fresh and sweet, reminding him of honeysuckle growing on the vine. She wore her hair down, and burnished, as if she'd just stroked it a hundred times with a brush. He wanted to dive his hands into its silk.

"The girls are cleaning their room. That's a rare happening around here, so I hope you'll give it its proper due."

She grinned, a real smile this time. Maybe it would be all right after all.

"I'll put your bag in the guest room. You'll be right across the hall from the twins."

She nodded her thanks, then saw Mrs. B. come in with a bundle of neatly folded laundry. Gabe saw her glance.

"I, uh, got a little behind this week. Mrs. B. is helping out," he explained.

"Behind? My, I'd say he was behind. Hardly a clean stitch in the house," Mrs. B. revealed.

"Twins make a lot of laundry," he defended, then escaped down the hall to the guest room.

And to see why the girls had been so quiet lately.

"Here, let me help you with that," Sabrina said, reaching for the stack of bathroom towels the woman held.

"My—no, girl. You just settle in. I dare say, you'll have your hands full enough with those two precious girls the next few days."

It was what Sabrina feared. The apprehension that had haunted her since she'd made the offer to stay with the twins returned full force. What if something happened to the girls while they were in her care? She knew very little about looking after children.

Oh, she knew their minds. She studied their actions—like a scientist hot on the cure for the common cold. But this was different. This was life. Real life. And she came ill equipped.

She stuck her hands into the pockets of her loose-fitting cardigan so Mrs. Benjamin wouldn't see they were trembling. She didn't want to admit that she was frightened, that she doubted her abilities. She would ruin Gabe's business trip. She'd been the man's last hope for a sitter, she knew. And somehow, some way, she'd get through this. They all would.

"Hannah! Heather! What do you think you're doing!"

It was Gabe, his voice coming from the kids' bedroom, and his tone intimated trouble.

Mrs. Benjamin and Sabrina glanced at each other in alarm, then both turned and scooted toward the sound of Gabe's wrath.

"Oh, dear," Mrs. Benjamin said worriedly. "I was supposed to be keeping an eye on them. The moment a body turns their back..."

She didn't finish the sentence, but she didn't have to. Sabrina knew what she was going to say—that without constant surveillance, those two were capable of getting into almost anything.

Sabrina *smelled* the problem before she got to the bedroom—and one whiff told her she'd unwittingly been an accomplice in this particular escapade of theirs. And it had to do with Wild Lilacs. The small sample bottle of perfume the girls had conned her out of the night she'd brushed out their curls.

She'd meant to get Gabe's approval of course, ask if it was all right, but she'd forgotten. His kiss, as she recalled, had knocked all thought of it from her mind.

"*Where* did you get this?" Gabe was holding his nose and the empty bottle of the offending perfume.

The two had apparently doused themselves with the stuff, as well as anointed their dolls with it. Sabrina wished the earth would swallow her up, but it didn't. She had to stay and face the music.

"S'brina," the two little girls admitted. "She said we could smell pretty for you."

Why didn't the earth cooperate!

Gabe's glance quickly shot to her and she knew it was time to explain.

Chapter Nine

"Gabe, I—I'm sorry. I don't know what else to say."

Sabrina turned her palms up in a gesture of helplessness. Gabe knew he should let her off the hook—but *damn,* that perfume was strong, at least in this quantity. They'd be smelling it for a month.

But he found he couldn't stay angry with her. Or his pint-size daughters. Not for long. And no harm had been done. Not really.

"We'll talk about it later," he told Sabrina. "I want to go over the *rules of the house* with you before I leave."

He herded the two girls toward the doorway and the bathroom down the hall to clean off the permeating scent. As for the dolls, perhaps he could dunk them in the bath as well to wash off the smell.

"No more playing with makeup of any kind without adult supervision," he told the two culprits, using his best authoritative voice.

"Yes, Dad," they chimed in unison, and Gabe's heart melted. It was hard to play the disciplinarian with them.

"Mr. Lawrence, you're going to be late for the airport," Mrs. B. warned. "I can get these two washed up. You and Miss Sabrina have things to talk over."

Before Gabe could object, the woman had the girls in tow, marching them through the door. When they'd gone, Gabe turned to Sabrina.

He didn't like the worry lines pleating her brow, the regret in her eyes. She was blaming herself— when *he* should have been watching the twins. Instead of keeping a vigilant eye, he'd been busy packing and taking care of a million and one last-minute details. Mrs. B. had been busy, too, trying to catch up on the laundry. And Sabrina had only just arrived.

The girls had merely taken advantage of an opportune moment—something the little minxes were very adept at, he knew.

"Sabrina, there was no harm done. I didn't mean to bark at them. Or at you. At *anyone*. Perfume washes off."

"Gabe, I—I guess I have a few things to learn about children."

She looked perplexed, a little lost.

"Hey, I think you're great with children. Don't doubt it, Sabrina. Hannah and Heather love having you stay with them. And I'm relieved. I won't have to worry about them—they'll be loved and looked after. What more could I want?''

Someone who knows what she's doing. Someone with a tad of mothering skills perhaps. But Sabrina kept these thoughts to herself.

If Gabe believed in her, she'd find a way to be the woman he thought she was. She wouldn't fail him. Or his little girls. ''Maybe you'd better show me this rules-of-the-house edict you talked about.''

''Ah, yes. Well, it's nothing big, but if I know the twins, they'll try to put something over on you. And you gotta be prepared.''

Gabe led her toward a bulletin board in the kitchen. He'd drawn up a checklist for her, indicating the twins' bedtime, what they liked to eat, what snacks they could have. He'd also listed the pediatrician's phone number and the number of the hospital's emergency room.

''Just in case,'' Gabe said when he saw her worried frown.

''I also wrote a quick note alerting the doctor that you have my permission to have the girls treated—if necessary,'' he added.

Sabrina seriously hoped no catastrophe occurred while the twins were in her care, that everything would be all right.

''If you need anything, Mrs. B. is right next door— at least for tonight. And of course, this is the number where I can be reached in Kansas City,'' he told her.

He'd placed it next to the emergency numbers and Mrs. Benjamin's. What did she have to worry about?

Nothing—nothing at all. Sabrina just wished she believed it. But she gave Gabe a brave smile anyway.

The girls came bounding into the room, fresh and sweet and minus most of the perfume's scent. Mrs. Benjamin had brushed their hair and straightened their hair bows, as well.

"We want to tell you goodbye, Dad."

Gabe grinned down at them. "Hey, are you hurrying me out the door?"

"Yes," came their answer. "S'brina's going to watch us now."

Sabrina smiled. Their vote of confidence made her feel a little guilty for her moments of doubt. Everything would be fine.

She'd just keep repeating that until she believed it herself.

"I'm hurt," Gabe said, feigning disappointment.

To Sabrina he winked.

The gesture, and his ensuing smile, curled her toes and sent a flush of heat to her cheeks.

He picked up his overnighter that Mrs. Benjamin had set in the front hall for him and started toward the door. His two girls trailed after him, demanding one last goodbye kiss. Gabe bent down and gave them big smooches.

The one he added for Sabrina held a different tenor entirely.

It was a man-woman kiss—and she still felt the aftershocks of it as he drove out of the drive, with one final wave to them all.

* * *

So far, things were going smoothly. Sabrina
couldn't ask for more. Except perhaps not to be reminded of Gabe on a constant basis.

Here in his home, where he was a part of every
room, it was impossible not to feel his presence. His
scent lingered on his worn leather chair in his den.
And in his bedroom—which she avoided except for
one tempting peek in. His daughters, too, were little
miniatures of the man she was beginning to care too
much about.

Mrs. Benjamin had finished up the laundry, and
while Sabrina helped her fold the last of it, they chatted about the twins, the neighborhood, her son and
daughter-in-law and her upcoming trip with them to
Estes Park. When the woman left, Sabrina realized
how alone she was with the girls. And on her own
with them.

Gabe phoned later that night to say he'd arrived
safely and to see if everything was all right. Sabrina
clung to his voice like a lifeline. Kansas City seemed
as distant as the other side of the moon right now.

"Don't let the girls con you into anything," he told
her in warning. "Pizza for dinner, ice cream, a half-
dozen trips to the park—all just a few of their little
gambits."

As Sabrina had learned. They'd had pizza for dinner already tonight. And she'd promised them ice
cream tomorrow. She'd try, however, to limit the trips
to the park to one—or two. Depending on how long
Gabe was away. She didn't tell him this though. It
would be their own little secret, hers and the twins—

though she suspected Gabe could guess. He knew his daughters only too well, it seemed.

"Look, we'll be fine," she told him. "Have a good meeting and don't worry about a thing."

His voice came back warm and trusting. "I'm not worried, Sabrina."

She'd needed to hear that. And wished she could feel the same assurance.

The twins chatted with their dad for a while—and happily did not mention the pepperoni pizza they had for dinner.

Or the promised trip to the Dairy Cone tomorrow.

Gabe would laugh and call her a pushover. And perhaps she was. Those two—and their father—had worked their charm on her, a charm she hadn't been able to resist.

A short while later she had the girls tucked into bed. They'd been strangely quiet since Gabe's phone call, and as Sabrina brushed back their soft curls, she asked them about it.

"What's the matter, sweeties? Are you missing your dad?" It would be only natural, she knew, for them to miss the man they'd come to depend on.

But she had the feeling this was something more, something that bothered them on a more threatening level, had them clinging to each other. No sibling rivalry tonight, just the two of them against the world.

"Wh-what if our dad doesn't come back?" Heather said, her eyes wide and solemn with the possibility.

"Yes...like our mom," her twin voiced, and Sabrina felt her heart break.

She thought of everything Gabe must have dealt with these past six months with his two little girls. How could she have thought *she* had all the answers? That she was the child expert?

Gabe had taken charge with them, had soothed their fears, dried their tears, given them hope and security when everything must have seemed lost to them.

Now they feared he, too, might disappear from their life, a fear Sabrina had to quickly put to rest. They'd been through so much. "Oh, sweeties—your dad will be back. I promise you that. He had some business in Kansas City. An account—like the one he did for the ice-cream store."

That seemed to put some reality into it, what their father was doing away from them, why he had to leave. And that he would be back as soon as he could.

"Will it be a d'zign for new ice cream?" Hannah wanted to know.

"And will we get some?" added Heather.

Sabrina smiled, wishing the two of them had had a life full of nothing but fun, ice-cream cones and trips to the park. Instead, they'd had to face sadness—and for that Sabrina hurt for them. "No design for ice cream. At least I don't think so, but he did promise to bring you a surprise when he came home," she reminded them.

The next few minutes they spent guessing what it might be—and Sabrina let their little imaginations run wild with the possibilities. Children's dreams were okay. It taught them to hope, to believe in something more, something wonderful. Taught them dreams could ride white horses.

She'd had such dreams once, and at times, she had them again—like when Gabe smiled at her, when he held her, kissed her.

"I think it's a new bike, a big one like Clarissa's," said Hannah.

"Nuh-uh. Bikes are too big to take on airplanes," scoffed her sister.

"Says who?"

"Says...*everybody.*"

Back to normal, Sabrina thought. The two fighting. She smiled in relief.

"Who's Clarissa?" she asked Hannah.

"She lives down the street."

"And she's grown up," added Heather. "She's *ten.*"

Yes, *ten* would be grown up.

"That's enough dreaming about surprises for now. It's off to sleep with you," she said, and gave them both a kiss on the cheek.

Not satisfied with that, they reached up and hugged her, then told her maybe their dad would bring *her* a surprise, too.

She smiled at the thought, though she didn't expect Gabe to remember her with any surprise. His presents would be reserved for Hannah and Heather—the two darlings who owned his heart.

Gabe had spent one restless night. First, he and Winfield had burned the midnight oil going over var-

ious ad campaigns—none of which seemed to be what
the man had in mind. When he finally got the chance
to return to his hotel for a few hours of much needed
shut-eye, Sabrina had filled his thoughts. He'd called
earlier, but he longed to call again, just to see how
she was, to hear her voice, so soft and sweet and thick
with sleep.

His hand had strayed to the receiver more than
once, but he'd stilled the urge to punch in the numbers. It had been nearly one—and he couldn't wake
her.

He'd tried to blot out her image and come up with
some ad gimmick that would please Winfield in the
morning—so he could be on his way back home. But
try as he might, all he could think about was Sabrina.
How soft and vulnerable she'd looked standing there
in his foyer that afternoon, a twin on either side of
her. How beautiful, with her hair tumbling over her
shoulders, her green eyes wide and a hesitant smile
on her kissable lips. Lips that kept him awake until
the early light of dawn, as he remembered their taste,
their silky feel, their feminine surrender beneath his.

This morning, he hoped to conclude his business
with Winfield and hop the first flight he could get
back to Denver. Back to his little family. What surprised him was that he considered Sabrina *part* of that
family.

When had it happened?

He was beginning to miss her and he looked forward to seeing her there in his home when he returned. Waiting for him. Welcoming him with her

smile, her sweetness. He'd never before needed a woman the way he needed Sabrina.

And it frightened him.

He wolfed down a complimentary roll and coffee in the hotel lobby and asked himself how it could have happened. He'd sworn off women—any woman. He'd been serious about his fatherly duty, dedicated to it. Then Sabrina had waltzed right past all that well-meaning resolve.

And if his restless night was any indicator, there was little hope of getting it back.

"I hope you've come up with something brilliant for me," Winfield said when he'd arrived at the man's office thirty minutes later.

"I have," Gabe answered.

He hadn't—at least not yet. But he'd wing it and hope inspiration would strike somewhere along the way. He wanted to return home the triumphant warrior, a hot thrilling kiss from Sabrina as his reward. He wanted to hold her in his arms, feel her perfect lush curves fitted against him and savor how good it felt to be back.

This trip had brought him to a new awareness, a surprised awareness of what he needed in his life. *Really* needed. And that need was one green-eyed, glorious woman, who thought she knew all about children, when what she really knew was how to subtly seduce him into falling for her—falling in a big way.

Sabrina took a cake out of the oven in Gabe's kitchen and slid it onto the countertop to cool. She

had the dinner for his homecoming ready and sim-
mering on the stove. Chili, his favorite—according to
the girls.

She'd even used his own recipe. She'd found the
little gem, dog-eared and splattered with chili sauce,
tucked away in an old cookbook, the writing his own,
some ingredients added, others deleted, as if the combination changed with each making. She hoped the
latest was accurate as she stirred the pot.

She'd made cornbread and prepared a salad to go
with it. Now all that was left to do was frost the cake
and perhaps pretty herself up.

The girls were setting the table with a minimum of
fighting and arguing about where to put the forks and
which side the napkins went on. Sabrina knew they
wanted everything to be right for their dad. So did
she. She wanted everything to be special, in fact.

She nervously checked her image in the mirror in
the hallway, tucking in a wisp of hair that had escaped
its soft twist at the back. Gabe would be here soon.
At least that's what she'd told the girls the last five
times they'd asked.

She hoped he'd be pleased that she'd done so well
with them. Everything had gone fine. There'd been
no catastrophe she couldn't handle, no squabble between them she couldn't referee.

Perhaps, just perhaps, motherhood wasn't such a
daunting proposition after all. Someday she might...

Might what? Have a family of her own? Forget her

fears of failing at marriage a second time and find a man she wanted to spend the rest of her life with?

When she thought of a man of her own, children of her own, the image that came to mind was of Gabe and the sweetest pair of twins she'd ever met.

But Gabe wasn't looking for a wife. He wasn't looking for a mother for Hannah and Heather. And Sabrina wasn't sure she could fit the bill anyway.

Two days of mothering two little girls wasn't the same as full-time motherhood. An evening of fixing chili and cornbread and one chocolate cake for the man she'd missed with a fury wasn't the same as being a wife.

She'd been only playing house here in Gabe's home. That was the *real* reality of these last two days here with Hannah and Heather. And it was what she shouldn't forget in the excitement of their father's homecoming.

Tonight she'd go home to her own apartment. Alone. And Monday she'd return to the institute, hand over the results of her study with the girls to Violet to type up. In time, these two darlings—and their father—would be only a memory. The two little brave sisters only a few pages in her research data.

And the realization of that made Sabrina's heart ache.

"Are you crying?" asked Heather, finding her holding back a spate of tears.

Sabrina tried a smile and brushed away the moisture that threatened to dampen her cheeks. "Crying?

No, I—I just got a little chili spice in my eye,'' she said and hoped Heather would believe it.

The little girl studied her for a long moment. "When we get something in our eye, Dad washes it out for us," she said.

"Well, that's good advice, but I think I'm fine now." She offered a smile to prove it, one she didn't quite feel. "How about we frost that cake?"

Both girls thought it a wonderful idea. Sabrina had committed herself to this welcome home for Gabe and there was no way out of it now.

Chocolate frosting and little girls didn't mix, Sabrina soon found out. Hannah had it on her fingers and on the tip of her nose, Heather had it down the front of her once-clean pink blouse before they were finished with the project.

It was back to the bathroom for a quick cleanup.

About the time Sabrina had them looking spotless again she heard Gabe's car in the drive. Both girls squealed with delight and raced to the front door.

Sabrina stole one last peek at herself in the mirror. Frazzled. It was the best word to describe her looks at the moment. Gabe would think his two angels had gotten the best of her for sure.

She tried to do some damage control, tucking in errant strands of hair, biting at her lips to evoke a little pink color.

There, that was better, she decided, and went to greet the man she'd missed these past two days.

He had a twin in each arm, swinging them around when Sabrina reached the front hall. Two sets of little-girl arms clung to him, and Sabrina resisted the urge to throw her own around his neck.

He saw her then, and paused midswing to gaze at her. She gazed back, wanting to take in the look of him. The twins had mussed his hair, which made him seem all the more endearing. He was a father through and through—what he'd wanted to be to his girls.

This was a happy family, a loving family, and Sabrina envied them that.

"We setted the table all by ourselves," Heather told him.

"And S'brina made chili and cake—just for you. But we get some, too," her sister added.

A softness stole into his eyes and Sabrina felt a smile tug at her lips.

"You did that for me?"

"Yes."

He put the twins down and took her into his arms. His kiss was warm and intimate—and Sabrina knew that the wall she'd been hiding behind had crumbled, knew that she had fallen in love with Gabe.

Chapter Ten

Over the next week and a half Sabrina saw Gabe and the girls often. Not in a professional capacity—she'd finished her research study with the twins when Gabe had been away. She had no real reason to extend the relationship any longer—except for the personal. The frightening, scary personal.

Most of the time the girls were along to keep things in some sane sort of perspective for her, but tonight she and Gabe were alone. Gabe had suggested the date, dinner at an intimate little restaurant, as a special thank-you to Sabrina for having saved the day—and his ad account—by staying with his daughters.

Sabrina hadn't needed any more thanks. He'd come home laden with surprises for the twins and a very beautiful surprise for her—a delicate music box that played a light whimsical tune. She'd placed it on the small table beside her bed and listened to it every night before she fell asleep.

"How about an after-dinner drink?" Gabe asked her, pulling her out of her thoughts.

She smiled. "None for me, thank you. I'm afraid that wine has gone straight to my head."

"Ah, perchance I can take advantage of the lady tonight." He waggled his sexy eyebrows at her, which made her laugh.

Gabe could do that to her. He could make her respond to him in so very many ways, on so very many levels—but tonight she wished she had a little better control of her senses.

He paid the bill, then escorted her from the dimly lit restaurant out into the cool summer night with its resplendent moonlight. From one romantic setting to another, Sabrina thought, but she doubted even broad daylight and a large brass band would be enough to provide distraction.

In the 4×4 she leaned her head back in the seat and tried to think of anything but the man beside her. Gabe, with his warmth and caring, his humor—and that infuriating male sensuality of his—made it difficult for a woman to turn her back on him, to beat a healthy retreat.

He'd waltzed into her life one quiet summer day— and turned her world upside down. And she doubted anything would ever be right again.

Not without him.

"A penny for your thoughts," he said as he walked her to her door.

The night breeze was light, the sky lit by a million stars. How easy it would be to tell him what was on her mind, how easy to slip into his arms and stay there forever, to let him make love to her, the way her body cried out for it with her every heartbeat.

But she couldn't tell him her thoughts, couldn't tell him she'd fallen in love with him. Schoolgirl, foolish love. Hearts-and-flowers love. Forever love.

"Too cheap," she said. "My prices come higher than a penny."

It was banter—anything to take her mind off the reality of the night, that she wanted to spend it with him—and every night for the remainder of her life.

"I'll take out a bank loan and get back to you."

He made her laugh. It was only one of the many things that made him special.

"Come in for coffee?" The invitation was out of her mouth too easily. But she didn't want the evening to end—not yet.

A smile lit his face, one a bit too satisfied, *dangerous*, as if she'd played right into his very male hands.

"The invitation was for *coffee*," she reminded him.

"Did I say a word?"

He didn't have to. Sabrina had read the signals and she'd felt the tension so very palpable between them—the wanting, the need.

She might not be all that experienced but she knew when a man wanted her—and Gabe did. If only for the night.

And Sabrina wanted him.

The only problem was one night would not be enough—not for her.

She directed Gabe to the living room and went to the kitchen to put on the coffee. She'd bought a new special blend she wanted to try. She hoped Gabe liked it.

Gabe feared he'd never be able to keep his hands off Sabrina. Tonight she had tempted his soul. She looked so very lovely in a slender black dress that hugged her every curve, exposed her neck—making him want to nibble its sweetness.

He dragged a rough hand through his hair. The tension had been there between them all evening, unspoken but clear just the same. Need, desire, want.

But it was more than just that—it was so much more.

Sabrina had captured his heart. In a way no other woman ever had before. His days were no longer his own. He was plagued by thoughts of her. His nights... *Those* could be summed up in one word: *torture*.

She confounded and confused him. One moment he wanted her in his life—on a permanent basis. The next he was swamped with doubts. He'd proved once he was no candidate for marriage.

The same could hold true a second time.

And what about the twins? He had to consider them in any equation of his life that involved the fairer sex. Sabrina would make a difference in their family. With the step taken, they could not return to the way things had been.

Damn, but this woman had done a number on him.

And somehow he had to figure out what to do about it—before he made some foolish mistake. Before he made love to Sabrina—the way he wanted to tonight.

She sauntered into the room, much the way she had into his life, his soul, into every fiber of his being.

"Sabrina…"

She set the tray holding two coffee cups on the table in front of the sofa, then gazed up at him. There was such softness, such promise, swimming in her green eyes. Her lips parted slightly, peachy and lush. He'd been about to tell her he had to go, that he couldn't stay for the coffee she'd made. Instead, the need he'd tried to conquer all evening ignited like a blaze in a paper factory, and he drew her to him. She fit there. In his arms. Soft against hard. Female against male. Sweetness against…

He couldn't think of a term to describe the heat in him, the crazy burning need.

She moistened her lower lip with the tip of her tongue as if in anticipation of the inevitable. He bent his head, closer, closer, until her femininity surrounded him, blotting out everything but the moment, the wonder of it, and the need that hummed between them, unfulfilled.

He went a little crazy, the world spinning out of control as he tasted her mouth, drank in the essence of her. Her lips parted on a deep sigh and he invaded her mouth, needing more—more of her, all of her.

It was what Sabrina knew would happen—and she'd been powerless to stop it. Was powerless now. Gabe owned her heart, all of her. His heart surrounded her, his body held her prisoner, a willing prisoner to whatever he wanted of her. All thought left her, save one. The love she felt for this man.

He groaned low in his throat, or had it come from her? She no longer knew. They were one, entwined by need, by want. It was dizzying and wonderful, and she wanted it to go on forever, wanted to stay here in his arms, wanted to know this man with her very soul.

But she knew that couldn't be—and Gabe knew it, too. He drew away, only slightly, but to her it was miles. Distance rushed in all too quickly.

He gazed down at her, the flame not at all extinguished in him. "I'd better not stay for that coffee, because if I do, sweetheart, I'll end up taking what I ache for."

Before the fog could clear from her brain, he turned and left. She heard the door close, and emptiness echoed through her apartment.

"Gabe, what have we done? And where is this going?"

Her words rang against the quiet in the room, and no answer came to her.

It was Saturday. Sabrina had promised to take the twins shopping for new clothes for school and she and the girls had been looking forward to it. For their first day as first graders they wanted something very special to wear, and had asked Sabrina to help them choose.

It promised to be a fun day—just the three of them.

At least she hoped Gabe wasn't planning on joining their little shopping spree. She hadn't yet sorted out what had happened between them the other night. The intensity of Gabe's kiss, and what she was going to do about this relationship she found herself in, with no seeming way out.

She hadn't wanted to fall in love with this man, but against all her better sense, it had happened.

By the time she arrived at Gabe's, the twins were ready and waiting for her. Not the usual matched pair of bookends this morning, she noted in surprise. Hannah had on red plaid and Heather wore blue denim. Hannah's hair was in a ponytail and Heather's in two big pigtails. Sabrina glanced up at Gabe, her mouth agape.

Never had she seen the twins in anything less than identical clothing, right down to their hair ribbons.

"This is all your doing, Sabrina. I hope you realize that."

Her eyebrows raised. "My doing? I'm not sure I follow."

He stood on the front porch, arms crossed over his chest, the toe of one loafer tapping a staccato beat against the top porch step. "They've decided they no longer want to dress alike. They want their *own* wardrobe."

Sabrina chuckled at Gabe's mock ferocity and gave the girls a thumbs-up sign. They looked adorable, dressed alike or unalike. But she liked unalike much better. She decided she could forgo relating her reasons. Gabe wasn't ready to listen to the news that his little girls were growing up, that they were growing more secure in who they were, that they no longer needed to cling to one another the way they had only a short time ago.

Sabrina would like to take some of the credit for that, but she thought the credit went to Gabe alone. He'd been the stalwart member of their little family, the port in the storm for his daughters.

It was only one of the things she loved—and admired—about him. And perhaps when they were alone she would tell him that.

He raked a hand through his hair. "Do you have any idea how much this is going to cost me—or had you thought about that?"

She laughed at his stunned-father routine. Wait until he had a pair of weddings to plan. How she wanted to be around to see that.

She sobered, realizing the truth of her thoughts. She did want to be around for Gabe, for the twins. She couldn't imagine life without them. But she was not a part of this family. Their lives would go on, and so would hers.

Somehow.

The twins giggled as their dad gave an exaggerated sigh and plucked several large bills from his wallet and handed them over to Sabrina.

"Why do I have the feeling this won't be nearly enough?" he asked.

Sabrina glanced up at him, then at the twins with a conspiratorial smile. "Oh, we women can be very frugal, can't we, girls?"

"Uh-huh," they chorused, not entirely sure what it was they were agreeing to.

Gabe looked askance. "I would think *frugal* and *woman* a contradiction in terms," he said with a snort.

Sabrina's eyes widened, then narrowed sharply. "You, Mr. Lawrence, are a chauvinist," she said.

"No, just a...*realist.*"

So was Sabrina. But she seemed to have forgotten reality these past few weeks. She pocketed the bills in her purse. "Sure you don't want to come along?" she asked, hoping that he did not. This was to be her day with the twins—and whenever Gabe was around he muddled her mind and definitely her senses.

"I'd rather have my fingernails ripped out—one by one," he offered.

He gave each twin a noisy kiss, and Sabrina a quick buss on the cheek—as if he didn't dare do more. At least not in the middle of the morning, on his sunny front porch. "Have a good time, ladies."

"We intend to have a wonderful time, don't we, girls?"

The two agreed wholeheartedly and waved goodbye to their dad.

They did have fun. Sabrina had been worried that their little legs couldn't keep up with all the mall walking, but the twins did beautifully. They'd shopped in every little-girl department the stores could boast of, buying more than they should have—and spending most of Gabe's money in the process.

Sabrina bought the first-day-of-school dresses herself, wanting to do something special for the girls.

She'd tried to talk them out of it, but Hannah and Heather had reverted back to identical—at least for that scary first day. But Sabrina wasn't worried about them. They would find their self-courage easily enough and soon settle into the school routine.

And once in a while it was nice to be a part of a whole, the other half of something special—like twin-hood.

Or marriage?

"How about lunch, girls?" she asked. "Are you hungry?"

They elected that they were, so Sabrina led the two tired shoppers toward the food court and bought them everything they wanted.

Today was special, after all.

The girls were quiet during lunch and Sabrina was curious. She'd caught their little blond heads together more than once today, as if they shared some giant secret, and Sabrina itched to know what it was.

Did she ask?

Or wait for them to open up on their own?

She and the girls had become friends. She felt it deep in her heart and knew they did, too. It made her feel good. Very, very good.

"How about a big slice of chocolate cake?" she asked.

Was this spoiling them? she wondered. She could understand how parents succumbed to the trap.

"I want a piece," announced Heather.

"Me, too," echoed Hannah.

Sabrina paid for the desserts, getting a slice for herself, as well.

"This isn't as good as *your* cake," announced Hannah.

"Yes, yours is better."

Sabrina smiled, pleased at their little compliment.

"Ask her," Heather said, nudging her sister in the rib cage. "Ask her—*now*."

Sabrina gave them both a questioning glance. Their blue eyes were wide and solemn in their little faces. She leaned forward over the table. "Ask me what?"

Did they want ice cream next?

Or had they seen something in a store that had caught their eye? Something they hadn't already bought?

Heather looked shyly up at her, Hannah more boldly. "Heather and I d'cided," the little girl said. She paused to frown at Heather wriggling on her chair.

Sabrina glanced from one to the other, certain something was going on here, but what she didn't know. "You decided what, sweeties?"

"That we want you to marry our dad."

"Yes," echoed Heather. "Then…then you can be our new mommy."

That was what they'd had their little heads together about.

How had they come up with this? And when?

Sabrina swallowed a lump in her throat larger than the state of Rhode Island.

Their little lives had been turned topsy-turvy recently. They ached and hurt inside. They wanted a family—all children did—but their little family had been smashed, first by divorce, then by something even more devastating.

Sabrina couldn't take their mother's place. No woman could do that. But to their little-girl thinking, Sabrina would be a giant bandage to the ache in their hearts.

What they didn't realize was that Sabrina had no experience with motherhood. She knew children—but in the impersonal. She knew behavior patterns, growth patterns, but that was something different. Far different.

She and Gabe had been playing with fire with this relationship. She should have known that—and put a stop to it before two small children got hurt. Hurt again, by life, by circumstances.

She shouldn't have gotten involved with a man who had two vulnerable little daughters.

"Oh, sweeties, I..." Sabrina didn't know what to say, how to tell them this couldn't be. "I—I'm flattered, but—"

"But you don't want to be our mommy?" This from Heather, a quiver in her small voice.

"Oh, no, honey. It's not like that...." Sabrina knew she had to do something, something she should have done a long time ago. Before any of them got hurt.

"I—I think your dad and I need to have a little talk."

She would have to end things with Gabe. Forget

the moments in his arms that made her feel so very special. It was time for her to face the truth of who she was and what she was capable of giving to Gabe and his two daughters.... And realize that she had to run away from the happiness of this little family.

Gabe tucked the twins into bed that night. They'd shown off their school clothes proudly. But there was something missing in their bright little eyes, something akin to the dazed glaze he'd seen there at their mother's funeral and during the long weeks following while they got used to Gabe in their lives again, got used to a new city, new friends and a life without their mother.

Sabrina had said only that she and Gabe needed to talk. Seeing the solemness and desolation in her eyes, he instinctively knew that whatever it was, it needed to wait until his little girls were in bed and he and Sabrina were alone.

"Can you leave the light on, Dad?" Hannah asked.

She hadn't made that request in many months now.

"Sure, pumpkin."

He kissed them both and exited the room, suspecting before he got halfway down the hall the two little girls would be clutching each other as tightly as they were the stuffed animals they slept with.

Whatever had happened today had been major and he needed to know what it was.

He found Sabrina on the sofa in the living room. She was perched on the edge as if ready to take flight.

He'd felt her distancing herself from him all evening. Why?

He knew now that he loved her, loved her with a heat that ran deep. The thought of marriage a second time scared the hell out of him but his mind had toyed with the idea nonetheless.

It could be good. Sabrina fit here in his house, in his arms. And she'd fit in his bed at night, a bed that had begun to seem horribly empty of late. But right now she looked small and fragile. And there was pain in her eyes that gave him a strange sense of foreboding.

He didn't go to her, as much as he wanted to. As much as he wanted to hold her, kiss her and make whatever it was that was bothering her—bothering them all—go away.

"I think you'd better tell me what's going on," he said.

She clasped her hands together so tightly, the white of her knuckles stuck out in stark relief. Her voice was soft when it came. Troubled.

"Hannah and Heather have...arrived at a grave misunderstanding," she began. "They...they think there's something between us."

And there wasn't? What did Sabrina think had been in his mind these past few weeks? When he'd held her in his arms? When he ached for more of her? He clamped his jaw tightly and forced himself to listen—to all of it.

"They think we...you and I...that we should get married."

Gabe's jaw relaxed and a small smile touched his heart.

That was it?

He wasn't sure he liked his little girls doing his proposing for him, but this was something easily remedied.

"I'm not sure what they read into this relationship was such a misunderstanding." He went to her and sat beside her. "I love you, Sabrina. I realized that while I was away, realized it more every day we were together after that."

Her head came up and he knew instantly that there was more, more she wasn't telling him. He tensed.

"You...you don't feel the same way, is that it?"

"Oh, Gabe." Sabrina hugged her arms to her body to stop the trembling. She loved him, too. So very, very much. She ached to tell him that, to fall into his arms, let him make this coldness she felt seeping through her go away.

He could do that, he could make everything right— except for one thing.

She stood up, not trusting herself to be too near him at this moment. She needed distance, needed to think clearly.

"Gabe, they...they want me to be their new mom. And...and I can't be."

The last words were spoken so quietly, Gabe nearly missed them. He saw the fright in her eyes, the fear of taking on two little girls who were his life, two little girls he'd made a commitment to, two little girls he couldn't fail—not a second time.

Sabrina saw she'd hurt him, hurt him deeply. He didn't understand, couldn't know the fear she felt. If marriage was a step a girl didn't take lightly, motherhood was a giant one. Attempting both simultaneously was...harrowing.

At least to her.

She'd failed at marriage with Phillip. He'd thought her cold and unfeeling. She'd only recently learned how to let her feelings out, to trust in them. Gabe and the girls had taught her how.

They'd pulled them from her one by one, until they were all out there, blowing in the wind, fragile and vulnerable.

And now it had brought her pain—pain she didn't think she could ever get over. It had brought all of them pain.

It took so very much to be a wife and mother. More than just love. It took feeling and warmth, a heart open to everything, including hurts. It took devotion and intimacy, a sharing of hearts and minds.

"I—I'm sorry, Gabe. But I...don't think we should see each other anymore."

He glanced at her and she saw the beginnings of fury in his eyes, a coldness that pierced her heart and left it bleeding.

He nodded. "I think you're right. I'm sorry I thought there could be anything between us, that I dared hope for more. I thought I'd seen love and caring in you, but you'd had your own agenda all along."

"My...my own agenda?"

"The twins—they fit nicely into your pet project, didn't they? And me—was I an intriguing subject, too? Single father raising twins alone?" He was lashing out at her. He wanted to hurt her the way she'd hurt him and his two daughters.

Gabe's words stung. It was what she'd felt in the beginning. She'd been intrigued by the dynamics of their family. Gabe was right. But she doubted she could make him believe that it quickly became more.

Hannah and Heather had captured her heart. And so had their handsome father. Research took a back seat to everything else. What she cared about was the three of them.

And what she'd lost was the three of them.

"I'd like to tell the girls. Explain—"

"Not tonight, Sabrina. I think we should both think this through before we inflict any more hurt on them."

The hardest thing Sabrina ever had to do was walk to the front door and out into the chilly night.

The hardest thing Gabe ever had to do was let her go.

Chapter Eleven

Sabrina's job at the institute had suddenly become more difficult. Every day she worked with children who reminded her every moment of two little girls—and of the man she'd given up.

The twins and Gabe had changed her in one irreconcilable way. She no longer knew how to work with detachment, with dispassion. They had made her feel. The irony of it was that what she felt now was pain. She missed them all with a fury, thought of them every moment.

Her small apartment had seemed so empty the night she returned to it. Quiet. She'd wanted to pick up something and hurl it against the wall, to rail against herself for her fear, her failing.

Gabe loved her. She'd heard his words. She hadn't realized how much she'd wanted to hear him say them until that moment. Sometimes when she was alone she replayed them in her mind and dreamed a different ending to that night.

But it always came back to her, the realization that it couldn't work for her and Gabe. She couldn't be the wife he needed. She couldn't be a mom for Hannah and Heather.

She tore her thoughts away and back to what was going on in the Play Lab. A set of two-year-olds toddled about, alternately chewing on blocks and banging them together. The two were not identical, but fraternal twins. She'd neglected this side of her study lately and needed to do more. But somehow she couldn't work up the necessary enthusiasm.

Perhaps in time…

Time. She'd always hated that phrase, *Time heals all wounds*. Did it? In this case she had big doubts.

Time could not make her forget Gabe, the feel of his kiss. Or what it felt like in the warm circle of his arms, to feel she was the center of his universe, the woman he wanted.

Time could not make her forget Hannah and Heather, their delight. The way they'd warmed to her and their very special friendship.

She knew she owed them an explanation. She had to give them some reason why she couldn't be in their lives anymore. But what? How did she explain to two little girls that adults got things so very confused sometimes. That they created problems they had no answers to. That life wasn't simple. It was complicated—and it hurt. The way they'd hurt so very recently themselves.

She hated that she was adding to their pain, but if she stuck around, and things didn't work out, how much more would they hurt? It had been the right decision to end it now.

She belonged *here*—at the institute. She had her work. And perhaps one day she would find the joy in it again. Perhaps one day the pain would glaze over.

One day she might even forget—just a little.

"Room mother?"

"Yes, Dad. The teacher said it was all right that you were a man," Hannah explained.

Gabe frowned. Just his luck! The two had a liberated nineties-style teacher who thought he had the makings of a room mother. "Does that mean I have to bake cookies?"

Heather brightened. "S'brina could help."

She said it as if that would solve it all. Gabe knew it would not.

"She doesn't want to be our mom," Hannah said. "I 'splained it to you, silly."

Hannah's words were tough, but Gabe knew it was big-girl bluff and bravado. He'd heard it from her often enough since Meg had died, knew that inside Hannah was hurting.

What did he say to them? How did he explain?

He'd brought Sabrina into their lives, then against his better judgment, fell in love with her. He hated it that the twins were paying the price. That should have been reserved for him. He shouldn't have let things go this far. Or this fast.

Not without considering the consequences.

He knew Sabrina was frightened—no, terrified—of her feelings. And he had known Hannah and Heather would tug on her heartstrings. And they had. He'd seen Sabrina's response to them. She'd begun to relax her emotions. He remembered how her face lit up at their smallest gesture of kindness, lit with amusement at their antics.

She'd warmed to him, responded with a hunger to his kisses, melted in his arms, trusting that he would not trample her heart.

He'd thought they could build something special together, thought Sabrina was the woman for him. The one rare woman who would fit in his little family and make it whole.

But she was too afraid, too afraid to trust what was there inside her, what he knew she had—a warmth and a beauty that ran deep. He'd felt it in her kiss, had seen it shimmering in her eyes—warmth, heat, caring. Love.

Only, when it was nearly out of the bottle, Sabrina had reined in those feelings so fast, Gabe was reeling from it still.

And so were Heather and Hannah.

"Kids, Sabrina…Sabrina has her reasons. Ones we don't quite understand. But…she cares very much about you. Remember what we talked about?"

They agreed that they did, but they didn't understand it any better than he did. That much was evident in their sad little smiles.

Sabrina had taught his daughters so much, taught

them that the memories of their mother were there for them to treasure, not to cry over…though that was okay, too. She had brought out their own special identities, taught them to revel in their differences, as well as their own special similarities—their gift of twin-hood. She'd done so much more for them than he had been able to do.

She'd taught the girls courage—but when it came to possessing it herself, Sabrina had chosen, instead, to run.

And that was such a tragedy.

"But, Dad, what about bein' room mother?"

Hannah brought Gabe back full circle. He needed Sabrina, her soft feminine influence in their lives—but he didn't have her. Wouldn't have her. It was up to him to make things right again. For all of them.

Maybe he could do this room-mother thing.…

"Don't take this as a yes…but I promise to think about it. Okay?"

Not quite the answer they wanted, he realized, but they nodded solemnly.

"Can we go play now?" asked Heather.

"Yes, dear hearts. Go play. Dad has to tackle some work in the den."

He had a business to run, a roof to keep over their heads. A life to live. Though all that would have been so much more rewarding with Sabrina—

Gabe nixed that thought before it went further. Sabrina wasn't in the picture—and by her own choosing. Life went on. He should have learned that by now. They all should have.

Just then the phone jangled and Gabe answered it on the second ring.

"Gabe..."

At the sound of Sabrina's voice his heart did a funny soft-shoe in his chest. Getting over this woman was going to be hard. Very hard, his gut reaction told him.

Her sweet face floated into his mind, refusing to be banished, no matter how hard he tried to do so. He saw the hesitancy in her as clearly as if she were standing there before him. He could see the green of her eyes, the lushness of her body, the way she moistened her lower lip when she was nervous.

And she was nervous now—he heard it in the crack of her voice, the rush of her words.

"Is—is this a bad time? Are you busy with the twins?"

What did she want?

Why was she calling?

"As good a time as any, I suppose. What can I do for you, Sabrina?"

There was a chill to Gabe's voice. Sabrina heard it, *winced* from it. For a moment she wished she hadn't called. Then she thought of the twins and knew this was what she had to do.

"Gabe, I—I'd like to see Hannah and Heather. I'd like a chance to explain—"

"Explain, Sabrina? I think you said it all clearly enough the other night."

No—she'd handled it badly and she needed to make amends. She had wanted to talk to them that night, to explain, but Gabe had discouraged it. And she'd abided by his wishes.

But that was then, this was now. "Gabe, I—I have to do this. Please...may I come by?"

"I don't want them hurt, Sabrina."

His words were harsh. And colder than the ice at the polar cap. She swallowed hard. "That's why I want to talk to them. I didn't want to hurt them either, Gabe. But I know I have."

Gabe held some of the blame, too—a great deal of it. He hadn't thought of the consequences to the twins—but now he was. "I'm not sure it's a good idea," he began.

"Please, Gabe...."

Was it something in her voice? The tremor in it that told him she was hurting, too? Gabe didn't know, but he felt his resolve begin to wane. Sabrina didn't have a cruel bone in her body. She cared about Hannah and Heather, he knew. He believed she cared about him, too.

Just not enough.

"I was planning to take them for ice cream this evening. If you care to join us..."

He heard her soft exhalation of air.

"Thanks, Gabe."

Sabrina didn't know how hard it would be to see Gabe again. If she'd tried to guess, she would never have realized how hard.

The moment she stepped inside the ice-cream shop, she saw him and her heart squeezed out an agonized beat. He sat at a back booth, smiling at something one of the twins was saying. That smile she knew so well. That smile she still saw in her dreams—and always would. She felt the tears sting her eyelids and she struggled for control.

Just then the girls saw her. They gave a hesitant glance at their dad, then soft smiles edged their lips. She stood where she was, unable to move.

Heather scooted from the booth to go to her and Hannah quickly followed. Gabe looked worried, concerned. She knew he didn't want his girls hurt—and Sabrina would do her best, her best to make them understand that the fault was hers, not theirs. Never theirs.

"We both made you something," Heather said shyly.

"From our first day at school," added Hannah.

The tears threatened again. "Oh, sweeties, I want to see it. And I want to hear all about your first day."

Gabe watched, hawklike, as she slid into the booth beside the twins. A mother bear protecting her cubs couldn't have looked more fierce.

"Hello, Gabe," she said nervously.

He only gazed at her, wariness in his look, as well as something else, something she interpreted as...regret.

Regret. She felt it, too. Her heart, her soul, wished things could be different.

"I'll go get our ice cream," he said. "It'll give you a moment alone with the twins."

A moment. Only a moment. There was warning in

his tone, his silent plea, "Don't hurt them," unmistakably loud.

She gave him a reassuring smile.

Two quiet little girls pushed first-day-of-school paintings toward her. "We made 'em ourselves. Just for you," said Hannah.

Sabrina studied the first-grade work, and tears came to her eyes. This time there was no holding them back. Four figures peopled the scene, two big ones, two small ones. Trees dotted the background and there was a big bright sun overhead.

"It's the day we went hiking," added Hannah.

"I see that," Sabrina said. In reality she could barely see anything through her tears, but she fought them back. "I have just the place to hang these masterpieces," she said. Her office was far too drab. And these would bring a warmth to it, a reality to it. Though it would hurt every time she glanced at them.

"Dad said that you still care about us, even though you don't want to be our mom," Hannah suggested hesitantly.

"Is it true? Do you love us?" asked Heather.

With every part of her being. "Yes, I love you both very, very much. Your dad was right about that."

The two glanced down at the table in front of them. Hannah played with her hands nervously. Heather picked at a small nick in the tabletop. It wasn't enough for either of them, their actions told her. It also told her they were trying to understand this strange confusion of adults.

How did she explain? What could she say that

would make sense to them—when none of it made sense to her? Still, she had to try.

"Sweeties, I know this is hard for little girls to understand, but sometimes adults' lives get...complicated. We can love someone very much, but we can still be...afraid."

Hannah's big blue eyes glanced up at her. Gabe's eyes. Accusing eyes. "But you told Heather and me not to be 'fraid. 'Member? That—that if we're brave, things turn out okay."

Words. Words meant to give courage to two little girls for that scary first day at school. Yes, Sabrina remembered. And now she heard them again. From the mouths of babes, she thought.

"Sometimes adults aren't as brave as little girls," she told them, sad that it was true.

Just then Gabe returned with the ice cream. He studied his children and then her. Sabrina answered him with her eyes, saying she wasn't sure her little talk had helped all that much, saying she felt so very, very lost.

Sabrina didn't even taste the ice cream, though Gabe had brought her her favorite—strawberry. The twins left half of theirs. Gabe, too.

As they stepped out into the quiet night, he took her arm. "You're a woman so full of love, Sabrina. A woman with a lot to offer. *Don't* hide from it forever."

That night, alone in her bed, she heard Gabe's words again. They tripped through her mind, taking root.

Hannah's words, too. *You told Heather and me not to be 'fraid.*

But the first day of school wasn't on a par with considering marriage, with taking that scary first step toward happily ever after. Or was it?

Big-girl courage or little-girl courage—how much difference was there?

Sabrina got up, tugging a blanket from the bed and wrapped it around her as she sat in front of the window, looking out. The fall night air had blown down from the mountains, sending Denver into its first cold snap of the season.

She shivered at the thought of how quickly winter would come.

Then spring.

Life, like the seasons, continued on. But would her life? Without the three people she loved most in the world.

She had so very much to think about. Courage to find.

Gabe loved her.

And, somewhere in that love, was the answer.

Gabe had tried working on a new ad campaign. He'd done the laundry. Hell, he'd even made an attempt to bake a cake, something he'd vowed never to try again after that sunken birthday cake for the twins.

All he could think about was Sabrina. And how empty his life felt without her. He walked through the house, hearing her silky laugh, her soft, feminine voice that had spoken to his girls, read them a story, discussed their fears.

He wanted to see her across the table from him at dinner, wanted to find her in his bed at night, wanted to wake up with her beside him every morning for the rest of his life.

The twins missed her. They asked about her all the time. Which didn't make it easy for him to forget the woman he wanted in his life, the woman who stayed just beyond his reach.

In the past few days, he'd gone to the phone to call her a dozen times or more, needing to hear her voice, needing that connection with her. But he always stopped himself in time.

Sabrina was afraid—afraid of her confounding feelings. And if he pushed, she'd run the other way, bolt like a skittish deer. She had to come to him. On her terms.

In her own time.

But it was hard to wait, to hope against hope that she would come—when everything suggested she wouldn't.

He'd worn a permanent path in the carpet in his den and an identical one in the living room.

The twins had come home from school today and gone straight to their room. They hadn't wanted a snack, hadn't even bit at his offer of a trip to the park. Tonight he'd done his final hat trick and ordered in pizza.

If that didn't work...

The pizza-delivery kid should be here any moment

and he hoped the aroma would pry his two little darlings out of their bedroom and back into his life. Without Sabrina it was damned lonely. With his two moppets moping about it was even worse.

He set out paper plates and napkins on the kitchen table and poured two big glasses of milk for the girls. A short while later the doorbell jangled.

"Get washed up for dinner, kids. Dad has a surprise for tonight."

Gabe went to the door and opened it. Unless Sabrina had changed her profession to pizza delivery this was not their dinner arriving. No familiar truck with a blinking light on top sat in the drive—only Sabrina's sensible blue-gray car.

"Were you expecting someone?" she asked at his attempt to glance around her.

"P-pizza," he managed.

"Sorry. Will I do?"

He didn't know what she was doing here, but at the moment he was happy just to stand there looking at her. She was so beautiful, she made him ache. Her hair tumbled over her shoulders. Gabe remembered its feel and longed to bury his hands in it. To drink in her fragrance, her femininity.

She wore a loose red cardigan sweater and slim jeans. A white blouse, opened a button or two at the top, revealed her creamy neck. He longed to plant a dozen or so kisses along its column. Instead, he invited her in.

She followed him silently into the living room. He didn't know what to say, and she seemed at an equal loss. She clasped her hands together, opened them, and finally clasped them again.

"Gabe, I'm not sure why I—I'm here. I mean, I do know—I guess what I'm saying is... Can we go back to the other day and...and that proposal of sorts you made to me?"

Gabe's heart thudded against his ribs. "Sabrina..." His voice held an edge, demanding an explanation of her, yet afraid it wouldn't be the one he wanted to hear.

Sabrina's heart beat in her throat. She wasn't sure how Gabe would feel. Perhaps he'd changed his mind about her. Perhaps she'd waited too long to find her courage.

"Gabe, I—I thought about what you said the other night. Thought about it a lot. And what Hannah said to me about...about being afraid.

"I have been afraid, Gabe. Afraid I was an authority on children—but only in theory. That in the practical I would fail. I was afraid I might fail in marriage. I had once."

"Sabrina..."

Sabrina put up a hand to stop him. She had to say this—while she still could, before her newfound courage evaporated.

"I never knew how to let my emotions show, to feel. My parents were never very demonstrative. They always had their work and I...I was sort of lost in the background. I hid my feelings. That cost me one marriage. And I was so frightened of failing a second time...with you. And with Hannah and Heather."

"I'd hoped all you needed was time, Sabrina. Time to realize how wrong you were."

"Wrong?" She glanced up at him, into his eyes that were so blue, so true. "I'm still not convinced I can do a good job at being a wife, a mother. All I know is that I don't want to be afraid to try. Not anymore. Oh, Gabe, you—and the twins—made me realize that. Do...do you still want me?"

"Do I want you? Oh, Lord—so very much. Marry me, Sabrina."

She didn't answer, couldn't get the words out around the big lump that rose in her throat.

"Do—do you want me to get down on my knees?"

He looked so serious she had to laugh. Gabe would do it—if she asked. She knew that. But all she wanted from him at the moment was to feel his arms around her—and a kiss.

"I love you, Gabe Lawrence—and yes, I will marry you."

Her answer sounded sweet to Gabe's ears. He took her into his arms and his hands found their way into the silk of her hair, his mouth took hers.

"*S'brina.*" The twins burst into the room, looking surprised and curious. "Is S'brina our surprise, Dad?"

Gabe laughed, not releasing his hold on the woman in his arms. "Yes, girls, I think she is."

The twins ran to them, demanding to be part of the hug, too.

"Are you gonna marry us, after all?" Heather asked.

"And be our new mom?" added Heather.

"Would you like that?" Sabrina bent down to twin level.

"Yes," they chorused in unison.

"Anybody here order pizza?"

Gabe glanced up at the unexpected voice coming from the vicinity of the front door, and the face peering in through the screen.

Pizza, damn!

He'd forgotten this had been his surprise for the girls, not Sabrina. But he was definitely pleased with the change in the agenda.

The pizza boy got the largest tip of the night, of the month. Possibly of his life.

Epilogue

"I love you, Mrs. Lawrence. Even if you are the size of Pike's Peak in your maternity clothes."

"Beneath these maternity clothes is your second set of twins. And if I'm as big as Pike's Peak, it's your fault."

He smiled. "And I had such fun getting you in that condition, too."

"Gabe... Oh, *Gabe*." The second *Gabe* came out in a gasp and his wife's hands flew to her protruding tummy. "I—I think you'd better get us to the hospital—fast."

"You mean..."

Sabrina gave a sigh. Men were so helpless when it came anywhere close to delivery time, and Gabe was proving her point. He raced around trying to locate the suitcase she'd had packed for five days now and sitting by the front door, hollering at Hannah and

Heather who came racing down the hall to ask if their baby brothers were about to arrive, and searching for the keys to the 4×4 that were on the hall table where he always dropped them.

Sabrina knew she would have to take charge—if she ever expected to make it to the hospital in time. But once the babies were born, Gabe would be the strong one again, taking care of all of them, the way he'd done with Hannah and Heather. He would again be the caring and loving and very capable dad she knew he was.

Calmly Sabrina walked to the phone and called Mrs. B. to come and stay with Hannah and Heather as arranged. She phoned her doctor to let him know she and the babies were on their way. Then she aimed Gabe toward the front door.

Matt and Mark were born two hours later. Gabe smiled down at his wife in the delivery room and brushed back a curl of her damp hair from her forehead. "Our sons are beautiful," he said. "*You* are beautiful."

Sabrina gave a tired, but very happy smile, pleased at the not-so-little family they had become. Her life was complete. It had come full circle. And she'd never known such happiness.

Emotions too numerous to absorb filled her at that moment, filled her, but no longer frightened her. She had lots of love to give and she intended to give it every day of her life.

"I love you, Gabe Lawrence," she said.

* * * * *

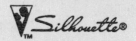

IN CELEBRATION OF MOTHER'S DAY, JOIN
SILHOUETTE THIS MAY AS WE BRING YOU

a funny thing
HAPPENED ON THE WAY TO THE
Delivery Room

THESE THREE STORIES, CELEBRATING THE
LIGHTER SIDE OF MOTHERHOOD, ARE
WRITTEN BY YOUR FAVORITE AUTHORS:

KASEY MICHAELS
KATHLEEN EAGLE
EMILIE RICHARDS

When three couples make the trip to the delivery
room, they get more than their own bundles of
joy…they get the promise of love!

Available this May,
wherever Silhouette books are sold.

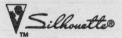
Silhouette®

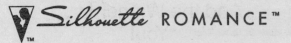
Silhouette ROMANCE™

cordially invites you to the unplanned nuptials
of three unsuspecting hunks and their

SURPRISE
BRIDES

Look for the following specially packaged titles:

March 1997: MISSING: ONE BRIDE by Alice Sharpe, #1212
April 1997: LOOK-ALIKE BRIDE by Laura Anthony, #1220
May 1997: THE SECRET GROOM by Myrna Mackenzie, #1225

Don't miss **Surprise Brides,** an irresistible trio of books about love
and marriage by three talented authors! Found only in—

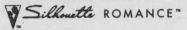
Silhouette ROMANCE™

SR-BRIDE

And the Winner Is... You!

...when you pick up these great titles from our new promotion at your favorite retail outlet this June!

Diana Palmer
The Case of the Mesmerizing Boss

Betty Neels
The Convenient Wife

Annette Broadrick
Irresistible

Emma Darcy
A Wedding to Remember

Rachel Lee
Lost Warriors

Marie Ferrarella
Father Goose

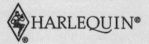 

ATWI397-R

As seen on TV!
Free Gift Offer

With a Free Gift proof-of-purchase from any Silhouette® book,
you can receive a beautiful cubic zirconia pendant.

This gorgeous marquise-shaped stone is a genuine cubic
zirconia—accented by an 18" gold tone necklace.
(Approximate retail value $19.95)

Send for yours today...

compliments of ▼ *Silhouette*®
TM

To receive your free gift, a cubic zirconia pendant, send us one original proof-of-
purchase, photocopies not accepted, from the back of any Silhouette Romance™,
Silhouette Desire®, Silhouette Special Edition®, Silhouette Intimate Moments®
or Silhouette Yours Truly™ title available in February, March and April at your favorite
retail outlet, together with the Free Gift Certificate, plus a check or money order for
$1.65 U.S./$2.15 CAN. (do not send cash) to cover postage and handling, payable
to Silhouette Free Gift Offer. We will send you the specified gift. Allow 6 to 8 weeks for
delivery. Offer good until April 30, 1997 or while quantities last. Offer valid in the
U.S. and Canada only.

Free Gift Certificate

Name: _____

Address: _____

City: _____ State/Province: _____ Zip/Postal Code: _____

Mail this certificate, one proof-of-purchase and a check or money order for postage
and handling to: SILHOUETTE FREE GIFT OFFER 1997. In the U.S.: 3010 Walden
Avenue, P.O. Box 9077, Buffalo NY 14269-9077. In Canada: P.O. Box 613, Fort Erie,
Ontario L2Z 5X3.

FREE GIFT OFFER   084-KFD
ONE PROOF-OF-PURCHASE
To collect your fabulous FREE GIFT, a cubic zirconia pendant, you must include this
original proof-of-purchase for each gift with the properly completed Free Gift Certificate.

084-KFD

Silhouette Romance proudly invites you
to get to know the members of

The Single
Daddy Club

a new miniseries by award-winning author
Donna Clayton

Derrick: Ex-millitary man who unexpectedly
falls into fatherhood
MISS MAXWELL BECOMES A MOM (March '97)

Jason: Widowed daddy desperately in need of some live-in help
NANNY IN THE NICK OF TIME (April '97)

Reece: Single and satisfied father of one about
to meet his Ms. Right
BEAUTY AND THE BACHELOR DAD (May '97)

Don't miss any of these heartwarming stories as
three single dads say bye-bye to their bachelor days.
Only from

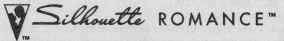

Silhouette ROMANCE™

Look us up on-line at: http://www.romance.net

SDC